Alone with the

Germans

gay tales from Berlin and beyond

Joseph Lavelle

Printed by CreateSpace,
an amazon.com company

ISBN-13: 978-1523316564

ISBN-10: 152331656X

Front Cover Photograph:
Joseph Lavelle, Brandenburger Tor,
West Berlin, October 1987
© Joseph Lavelle

Back Cover Photograph:
Joseph Lavelle, Cafe Melita Sundstrum,
Kreuzberg, Berlin, 2006
© Joseph Lavelle

Für Michael M.,
Alte Kuh gar leicht vergisst,
dass sie ein Kalb gewesen ist

Contents

Toll

Toll

I was dreaming. I can't remember what I was dreaming about, but I thought that the children's voices were part of the dream.

'*Er schläft,*' a girl said.

'*Nein, er ist tot,*' a boy insisted, then there were whispers then laughter and then, after a moment, soft, warm, little fingers stroked my cheek. I groaned, confirming that I was not dead as the boy claimed. The children screeched and, retreating from me, their feet pounded on the wooden floor. I opened my eyes and raised my head. Through the slowly closing bedroom door, I glimpsed them in the bright hallway, a mass of fleeing colour; fair hair, matching yellow t-shirts, his green shorts, her blue skirt, pale pink legs, white socks and red trainers. They were five or six years old, maybe older, I wasn't sure.

The door shut, throwing the room into shade. Hungover, I pulled myself up. I was in a double bed, a strange bed. Yet, for a few moments, I was confused, because I own the same blue and white Ikea duvet cover that stretched out before me. Then, of course, the realisation that I wasn't at home fully kicked-in – not just

3

Alone with the Germans

the children, but the unfamiliar wardrobes, the high
ceiling with its chrome light fitting and the tall, shrouded
windows. Sunlight seeped through gaps around the long
green curtains and the room smelt of bodies and sweat.
On the floor, I noticed my clothes in a heap and on the
bedside cabinet next to me, an alarm clock ticked.
Outside, traffic rumbled along Schönhauser Allee.

The events of the previous day came back to me - my
arrival at Schönefeld Airport then the taxi to the hotel
then check-in then a shower then dinner and then the
bar, the bar where I met *him*. So, where was he? Not
knowing concerned me, but I felt more uneasy about the
children, whose presence posed questions that I didn't
want to consider.

'I need to get out of here,' I thought. I was about to
climb out of bed when there was a sudden commotion on
the other side of the bedroom door. I heard the boy,
demanding and upset, holler. Then above his yell, I
heard a woman's voice. 'Udo, *halt dein Schnabel,*' she
commanded. The boy duly shut up. The girl said
something then the woman said something, but their
voices were low and I couldn't make out a single word.
The children then headed away from the bedroom, the
sound of their stomping on the wooden floor gradually
receding. I sighed, but then heard other footsteps,
lighter and more precise, approaching the bedroom. After
a moment, there was a knock on the door. The woman
then uttered a string of syllables in a sweet, high voice. I

understood nothing except her first word, '*Hallo.*'

'*Hallo,*' I replied.

The bedroom door opened. She peered from behind it before taking a few steps into the room. She was younger than I expected, perhaps seventeen or eighteen years old. She was tall and slim with small, high breasts. She wore a plain white, loose summer dress with strappy, white sandals and her bare arms and legs were pink. A white ribbon held her long, dark hair away from her pretty, oval face. She was not wearing make-up and her complexion was sallow, flawless. She smiled and her smile caused me to gasp. Her thin, pallid lips parted to reveal white, even teeth. It was a pleasant smile, a genuine smile. In fact, it was a beautiful smile. More than that though, her smile was *his* smile. Just as her eyes, deep brown and flecked with hazel, were his eyes too. Yet, her other features - a small, thin nose and dainty, rounded chin, weren't his at all.

Behind her, the door remained open and light from the hallway illuminated the room. She stared down at me, taking me in. I pulled the duvet further up my naked body. She glanced at my clothes on the floor then said something. I didn't understand a word. In the silence that followed, I realised that she was waiting for an answer. '*Wie bitte?*' I said at last.

Her brow crumpled and her smile became a frown. 'I was apologising for Udo and Inka,' she said. 'They should not have been disturbing you.' She smiled again. 'Are

Alone with the Germans

you American?' She sounded vaguely American herself.

'English,' I replied, repositioning myself.

Her smile lessened. 'You live in London?'

'Liverpool,' I said and the corners of her mouth dropped further. 'Have you heard of Liverpool?'

'Of course!' she exclaimed. 'It is the home of All We Are.' I had no idea what she meant. She read the fact on my face. 'A band,' she explained. 'They are very good.'

'Do you know the Beatles?'

She screwed up her face. 'Everyone knows of them,' she said. 'Not my thing though. They are the thing for my grandparents.' We looked at each other for a moment and then she advanced toward me holding out her left hand. 'I am Ania,' she announced. I leaned forward and took her long, slender fingers in mine. Her skin was warm and soft, her nails short and unadorned.

'Joe,' I said. We shook hands then she stepped back. 'Ania is a pretty name.'

'Thank you.' She smiled. 'It is Russian.' We looked at each other again. She broke the silence. 'He has gone out.'

'Out?' I asked.

'Yes, we need things, *Brötchen* and cold cuts. He also walks Lumpi, our dog.' She took a breath. 'He will return in some minutes.'

'Okay,' I nodded.

She placed her hands on her chest then smiled his smile again. 'I must be saying that I am so very happy to

6

meet you,' she gushed. 'He said about you, of course, but he said so little. Not even your name and yesterday, he was so very concerned about meeting you at the restaurant.'

I pulled a face. 'The restaurant?'

Midnight. A bar. A matt black bar - walls, ceiling and woodwork painted black. The all-male clientele is a mix of types, but mostly the over-30s in jeans and t-shirts. A few men are in gear; black leather, of course, or else rubber. Others - the younger set, wear jogging pants and branded trainers.

Me? I am the denim and t-shirt type.

I stand and nurse my third beer of the evening whilst watching a porn video playing on a screen high up on a wall. After a while, I grow bored and watch the locals instead. They take cruising seriously. No one smiles. No one drums fingers or taps a foot to the loud, incessant dance music. Most men are static, but a few traipse back and forth between the bar counter and the darkroom at the other end of the space. Everyone watches everyone else, but no one stares too directly, too intently; the night is young and there might yet be someone better looking or more their type.

I sip my beer then *he* walks into me. '*Bitte,*' I say, because, despite two terms of 'German for Business' and several night school classes, my *deutsch* is still lousy and I don't know how to say, 'Hey, stupid! Watch what you're doing!'

Apart from another man who has matched his black leather outfit with red trainers and a brown leather belt, he is the only man that I consider inappropriately dressed. He wears jeans, which are fine, but with a striped shirt that I would only ever wear to the office and a too-formal tweed jacket. Similarly, his shoes are patent leather slip-ons.

He realises that I am (if not English) an English-speaker. 'I am so very sorry', he says aghast in a heavy German accent. He holds a half-empty beer glass; the missing beer is on my t-shirt and the floor.

'It's okay,' I say, brushing at my chest and then I look into his face. His big, brown, bovine eyes captivate me; his irises flecked with what might be gold. He has a head of short-cropped fair hair that is thinning on top and greying at the sides. He wears a short, neatly-trimmed beard. His nose is wide and prominent. He has a strong jaw and a lined forehead. His lips are pale and narrow and guard neat, white teeth.

Despite my sartorial judgements, I'm suddenly transfixed and it's obvious that he's as much taken by me as I am by him. He's a little drunk and so am I, but I guess that I'm not as drunk as him - at least, I've not walked into anybody.

'I must buy you a drink,' he says. 'I am causing this accident of you.'

I counter the urge to correct his English. 'It's okay,' I

8

say, but my glass is almost empty and he insists so I allow him to buy me a beer. A little later, I reciprocate.

His name is Jens. He lives nearby, but isn't one for bars. 'Tonight I had some plans,' he explains. 'But... well, it went not as I was expecting. I needed a drink and here am I.'

'What happened?' I ask.

'I don't wish to talk about it,' he says. 'Do you mind?'

I don't. Instead, we talk about me and what I am doing in Germany - the sales seminar in Erfurt.

'How long are you in Berlin?' he asks.

'Tonight,' I say.

'Only tonight?'

'I return on Thursday for my flight home on Friday.'

'I see,' he says.

'You did not meet *Vatti* at the restaurant!'

'*Vatti?*' I asked.

'*Vatti*, my father,' Ania said.

'Jens?'

'Yes,' she said.

'No,' I said, 'we met at a bar.'

'A bar?'

I nodded. 'A bar.'

'You were not on a date?'

'No.'

'Oh!' she said.

'What's wrong?' I asked.

Alone with the Germans

She thought about it for a moment, sucking at the inside of her cheek. '*Nichts,*' she announced eventually. 'Everything is *toll*. You know this word *toll*, what means fantastic?' She giggled. 'Yes, things are *toll*.' She smiled his smile again. 'Would you like coffee or perhaps tea*?*'

'Coffee *bitte,*' I said.

'How do you like it?'

'With milk.'

'I will be just a little moment,' she said then left the room, closing the door behind her.

I hauled myself out of bed intent on getting dressed and out of the place. First, though, I opened the curtains. Bright sunlight poured in, hurting my eyes. When they readjusted, I noticed a colour photo in a frame. It sat on the cabinet on the other side of the bed. For some reason, I picked it up and studied it. The frame was metallic, but light. A black card mount surrounded the photo and seemed to make the colours especially vivid.

The photo showed Udo, Inka, Ania, Jens and another man. They were all smiling and sitting at a white table. Jens wore a yellow t-shirt and sat on the extreme left with Inka on his lap. Ania sat next to him, commanding the middle of the image. The other man sat to her right. Dark-haired and handsome, he wore a blue vest that revealed muscled arms and sculpted shoulders. Udo sat on his knee. The photo confirmed what I suspected about Inka and Udo; they were twins. They appeared to be about three or four years old and wore matching orange

10

tops. Ania wore a white t-shirt and appeared boyish; her chest was flat and she had a pair of sunglasses pushed up into short, flat hair. Jens looked as he had in the bar, the same short-cropped hair and well-kempt beard, only his face seemed a little fatter. The other man drew my interest; he appeared to be about my age with my colouring; early forties with dark hair, suntanned skin and brown eyes. We shared a similar build (although I admit to being less gym-honed).

I imagined myself in his place at the table and the questions that had seemed too daunting minutes earlier entered my head. Was Jens the father of Ania and the twins? That seemed probable – in the photo, they all had his eyes and smile. Were the children from a relationship with the same woman? Or perhaps there was more to it than that? After all, Ania was older than the twins. She was also dark-haired while they were fair. What significance did that have? Had there been two mothers? Had a surrogate been involved? And the other man, where did he fit in?

Outside the bedroom, Ania's footsteps interrupted my thoughts. I replaced the photo then climbed back under the duvet. She knocked on the door. 'Come in,' I said.

She entered carrying a red mug. 'You have opened the curtains,' she noted. The door closed behind her. '*Eine Tasse Kaffee,*' she declared.

'*Danke,*' I said taking the cup from her.

She boldly sat on the edge of the bed next to me.

Alone with the Germans

I took a sip of coffee then placed the cup on the bedside cabinet. '*Schmeckt gut*,' I said.

'Thank you,' she replied. She smiled, but her tone became serious. 'Do you mind if I ask something?'

'It depends what the question is.'

My answer discouraged her. She frowned and thought for a moment, but then she just blurted it out; 'Do you like him? I mean do you *truly* like him?'

'I like Jens,' I replied and she immediately beamed. 'But,' I added, 'I am not looking for anything serious and I am seldom in Berlin.'

'Oh,' she said, lowering her face. She sniffed and when she raised her head again, her brown eyes were wet. '*Vatti* is so lonely and you are the first since...' She paused, but then abandoned the sentence. Drawing another breath, she said, 'We want him to be happy. You understand?'

'Of course,' I said.

She sniffed again and would have said more, but out in the hallway, we heard feet on the wooden floor and then the bedroom door flew open. Red-faced and tearful, the boy entered the room.

'Udo!' Ania exclaimed.

He ignored her. '*Er ist nicht Christoph! Ich haße ihn*,' he screamed. '*Ich haße ihn!*'

'Udo! *Mach dein Mund zu*,' Ania commanded. She wiped her eyes then stood up. Udo fled and she went after him, but stopped at the door. 'I am sorry,' she said.

Toll

'Udo is a little upset. He says that he hates you, but how can he hate you? He does not know you.'

Jens pulls me into him. I offer no resistance. Our lips meet. His mouth is warm, soft, moist. Through our clothing, I feel his heart beating and his erection shifting. We unhitch a moment. He studies my face then smiles. It's a great smile, a genuine smile. In fact, it's a beautiful smile. He makes to say something, but hesitates. I look at him. 'What?' I ask.

He swallows. 'Would… would you like to sleep with me?' he says.

A strange question to pose in a sex bar, don't you think? Strange, but welcome.

Smiling back at him, I chance a little German. '*Ja,*' I say. '*Ich will das.*'

Outside, in the hallway, Udo sobbed. The girl said something. '*Danke* Inka,' Ania said.

I got out of bed and pulled my clothes on. Sitting on the edge of the mattress, I took a mouthful of coffee. I listened for a moment, but couldn't make out what they said. Then I heard Jens's voice and the clamour of paws on the wooden floor. The dog barked and there was more crying. I sighed and shook my head. Jens, his voice deep and masculine, said, '*Was ist los?*' Ania explained things. Jens comforted Udo, '*Kleiner Mann.*'

The dog barked again and I heard it pad along the

hallway before it pushed through the bedroom door. A small black dachshund, Lumpi sniffed the air then raised a front paw, holding it above the ground for a moment like a gundog that had discovered grouse. I stared down at him. 'Hello fella,' I said then Lumpi took a step closer, wagging his tail.

Outside the bedroom, things seemed quiet. I took a deep breath, put my jacket on then entered the hallway. Lumpi followed me, but scampered off somewhere.

The door to the kitchen was on the left. They were all in there. Inka and Ania sat at a table. Jens stood, leaning back against a cupboard, and held Udo in his arms. Udo hid his face in Jens' shoulder, but the others stared at me with their big, brown eyes.

'You are leaving!' Jens said.

'Hmm,' I grunted.

'*Er ist wie* Christoph,' Inka noted.

'*Ja,* Inka *das stimmt,*' Ania agreed. Udo suddenly looked up. His eyes, watery and red-rimmed, watched me intently. In her seat, Ania turned to face me. 'Do you understand what Inka says?' I did, but she spelled it out anyway. 'She says that you are like Christoph, the man in this picture.' She pointed at a framed photo on the wall; it showed Jens and the same man that appeared in the family photo in the bedroom. The two men stood side-by-side, smiling, wearing matching suits.

'Have you hunger?' Jens asked.

I nodded.

14

'Then eat with us,' he said.

I hesitated.

'What is it?' he asked.

'It feels ... complicated.'

'Because of the children?'

I nodded again.

'Sorry,' Jens said, 'I should have been mentioning them last night.'

Ania looked from her father to me. 'But Joe it is only as complicated as you make it,' she said. 'Udo has been upset and now he is once more happy.'

I frowned.

'You have hunger and we would like you to breakfast with us,' Jens said. 'Nothing else.'

'*Wir essen Toast und Marmelade*,' Inka announced. She paused for a moment. '*Und auch Müsli,*' she added.

'So, what do you say to it?' Jens asked. 'Toast and jam and muesli.'

'*Und Brötchen*,' Udo added unexpectedly, earning a pat on the back from his father.

'Yes,' Jens said. 'We must not forget the *Brötchen*.'

'Or the cold cuts,' Ania said, giggling, which brought on laughter from her brother and sister.

'*S*o toast and jam and muesli and *Brötchen* and cold cuts,' Jens said. 'How does that sound?'

Smiling, they all stared at me.

After a moment, I relented. '*Toll*,' I said. 'That sounds *toll*.'

shaun-how-sir-alley

bill's a smiler. most times i like that but sometimes it does my fucking head in. like when i'm coming down off something and it's 6 in the morning after sissyfucks or whatever the club's called and we're on some street corner freezing our tits off 'cause our t-shirts are sweat-stuck to our skin and there's a freezing wind and bill's in my fucking face fucking smiling.

- you alright ben he says
- fuck off bill i say
- ben's on a bad roll he says

he says it to the kraut who latched on to us. the kraut who takes his tank top off and whose skin becomes goosebumps and looks like sandpaper only without the shiny bits.

- hey ben. you okay ben the kraut says

he says it in a crappy american-kraut accent which just kinda makes me feel worse. and bill's beaming in my face and the world's turning too fast. and the atmosphere is too heavy and pressing down on me. and there's an acidy chemically metal taste in my spit and my tongue sticks to the roof of my mouth. and my stomach feels small. and there's some vein throbbing somewhere inside my fucking skull and i just wanna be alone. on my own. i need to crash. and i start crying. and even though he's holding me and though i can't see his face i know that bill's still fucking smiling.

like i say though. most times i like that bill's a smiler.

i think i love bill.

i think bill loves me.

i think bill loves everyone. that's why he always smiles.

once. when i was a kid. i had a dog like bill. a black labrador called sam. sam loved everyone too. stupid mutt got run over by a car though. and anyway what i really wanted was a dachshund. a sausage dog. i wanted a shorthaired brown one like the one that's on a leash being walked by the bint in very yellow hot pants as me and bill stand in the sun outside the hostel smoking weed in our boxers.

- *sind sie amerikaner* she says

high sweet voice. red hair. great face. no tits. wide hips. green eyes that lock on to bill's. he sucks on the spliff and smiles his smile and she smiles back at him. then she does this thing with her lips and her eyes and a finger and a lock of her hair. i override the urge to puke and kneel down to stroke the dog.

bill shrugs his shoulders.

- *engländer* i say

and then i stand up and kiss bill on the lips. and she pulls a gob like her dreams just turned to shite. and then she walks off but she looks back. and i look at bill and bill looks at me. and we laugh. and then the dog barks and she turns away and the dog turns away and then they're gone.

- what did she want bill says
- thought we were yanks
- why
- our boxer shorts
- how'd you know these things he says

and i say that i just do. and he says that i understand the lingo. and i say that i don't but he says that i kinda do and at least i can say the street names. he's right. i can. and he says he can't even say the name of the street we're on.

- schönhauser allee i say

and he tries to say it but he's fucking hopeless. and i laugh but he doesn't. and i think that for someone who smiles a lot bill hardly laughs at all which is weird don't you think. and i draw on the spliff and i think a mo.

- remember shaun from school i say
- tall shaun he says
- yeah i say
- what about him
- what did he always used to say in maths class

bill just stares at me.

- to that auld arse. mister fucking todd
- how sir bill says. he always used to ask how sir

it takes a few seconds for the penny to drop.

21

Alone with the Germans

-    shaun-how-sir he says. that it. shaun-how-sir-alley
and i draw on the spliff.

-    you're fucking genius he says

but i'm not genius. not really 'cause it ain't right. it ain't
how a kraut would say it. if nothing else alley and *allee*
aren't the same. it'll do though.

i take the spliff from him and take a deep draw.

-    our last night he says. shite ain't it

-    yeah i say

-    we should do berghain tonight

-    nah i say. we'd have to queue

-    that's okay. we queued last night

-    i can't be arsed with the big clubs any more

-    something proper gay then he says

-    like what

-    dunno. an underwear party. that'd be horny

-    see how we feel eh i say

-    got fucking work again on monday. gonna be on lates
     all week again. i need something big

i take another draw on the spliff then he takes it back.
and he sucks on it long and hard. and next thing the guy
from the hostel's there. so bill stubs the spliff out on the
wall. the guy from the hostel tells us to go inside 'cause
we shouldn't be standing on the street in our underwear.
and so we go back inside like good boys.

and i think that the guy from the hostel hates us. not
sure why he hates us. could be 'cause we're english.
could be 'cause we're younger and better looking than

him. could be that someone complained. could be that he just hates his job like we hate ours. could be he's gay or bi or something and not out and we're too much. too in your face. too camp. too queer. too whatever. could be he's constipated from all the junk food he eats while he's sat behind reception where he's always sat. could be that he hates us 'cause of something else. who knows. who cares.

we go back to bed. we sleep until eight then bill gets all horny but i ain't having any. so i get up then he gets up.
- not seen any sights or anything since we've been here he says. not even the brandenburg fucking gate and every twat sees that
- never came here for the sights i say. and anyway you can see the tv tower from here
- big fucking deal he says
but it really is a big fucking deal. it's fantastic. futuristic. still space age even though it was built in the fifties or sixties or something.

it's still light when we go to mcdonald's on shaun-how-sir-alley.
- you ok he says
- yeah i say
- only you got a gob like a smacked arse
and i think a mo.
- ever loved somebody i say

23

Alone with the Germans

\-   dunno he says. maybe

he takes the lettuce out of his bun and wipes the sauce off his fingers with a napkin.

\-   it's either yes or no i say

\-   that'll be a fucking no then he says

and he stuffs his burger into his gob. and chews it. and when he's swallowed it he looks at me.

\-   what about tonight he says

but i'm not really listening anymore and so he says it again. and i agree to do the underwear party that's on the flyer that he's got from somewhere or other.

so after mcdonald's we buy new pants at some gay place on shaun-how-sir-alley called bruno's. i go for calvin kleins. black briefs with a red waistband. the words calvin klein in white letters against the red.

bill goes for barcode berlin but not pants. a jock in green.

\-   you'll show your bare arse i say

he just smiles.

we spend 50 euros. can't afford it. not really. none of it. not the pants. not easyjet. not the hostel. not the clubs. not the booze. not the drugs. we've used my credit card for most of it. it'll take months to repay. it's amsterdam all over again. i need a better job. the warehouse pays fuck all and i hate it anyway.

i think about this stuff.

i think about it all the time. not sure bill ever does but how'd you know behind that fucking smile.

shaun-how-sir-alley

*

we walk back to the hostel. it's getting dark. there are cyclists and pedestrians and cars trams buses and a funny yellow train. we pass cafes that double as restaurants and cocktail bars. no place is just one thing here. they're cafes for breakfast then they're restaurants for dinner and tea. and after that they're cocktail bars for the late night boozers. they're all at it. the vietnamese. the italian. the thai.

bill wants a drink. so we go into some place. bill asks for ginger ale. the barman looks at him like he just laid a turd on the floor.

-   don't understand man he says

another crappy american-kraut accent. bill points at the ginger ale in the fridge.

-   ach ghin-ger alla the barman says

i laugh and the barman pulls a gob.

i can't decide what i wanna drink. i make a thing of it. get him to suggest something. he suggests bionade.

-   it is *bio* he says. what means organic. it is a new thing. a now thing. a german thing. it offers different flavours

-   what flavours i say

and he has to look at the bottles and translate for me.

ingwer-orange = ginger and orange.

litschi = lychee.

kräuter = herb.

-   what flavour will it be mac he says

25

Alone with the Germans

-   i'll have a beer instead i say

he gives me daggers but serves me anyway. i wink at him. and when we leave i pay up but don't tip.

back at the hostel me and bill shower together in the communal bathroom. we play around. and he screams and squeals and laughs for once but then he wants to fuck and i don't. he moans about it but we only ever fuck when he wants to fuck. and he's always top even though he reckons he's vers like me. only he never says vers or versatile. he says flip as in flip-flop. really though it doesn't matter what he calls it 'cause he's only ever top. and sometimes i'd just like him to be bottom. he is with other guys. that's what he reckons. so why not with me.

and then in our room i pull skinny jeans over my new calvin kleins. and bill watches me.

he reckons skinny jeans are a berlin thing like the thing for leather is a berlin thing. and the thing for full beards and sex bars are berlin things. and he's right but you get all those things in other places too. so how can they be the only things that make berlin berlin.

and then bill looks at the flyer for the underwear party.

-   do you keep your shoes on
-   dunno i say

and that night we're ready way too early and bill's still horny so we go to the sex place on shaun-how-sir-alley. it's a cinema. lots of screens. lots of booths. a screen in every booth. hundreds of porn movies. thousands maybe. you press a button at the bottom of the screen to flip through them.

the booths have cushioned leatherette seating and wood-effect melamine surfaces just like in mum's old kitchen. easy to wipe down i suppose. there're holes in the walls between some of the booths too. the edges of the holes are smooth and rounded. no chance of splinters in your dick.

i buy the beer. it's cold and tastes bitter.

there're only us and a few auld krauts in the place. bores me but bill likes the attention. they like his youth. his horniness. his smile. they follow him around the place. i sit on a sofa and wait. then bill stands near the entrance of a booth. he leans against the wall and exchanges stares with them. an auld kraut enters the booth and bill watches him. it looks like bill'll join him but he has second thoughts. he joins me on the sofa instead.

- no one worth doing he says
- you fucking prick-teaser i say

he just smiles and sups his beer.

then he gets a text on his mobile. you're not supposed to take mobile phones beyond reception. there are signs about it and lockers for your gear but who gives a fuck.

- someone's asking if we're still meeting up
- who i say
- dunno someone called t
- t

Alone with the Germans

- yeah the fucking letter t he says
- ah yeah i say. the kraut from sissyfucks

the kraut's name is thom. tom with an aitch. thom as in thom barron the porn star. thom barron the german porn star who's on some of the screens in some of the booths. but tom with an aitch is better looking than thom barron. younger. thinner. less pumped. more natural.

- yeah i remember now bill says. he wanted to meet at a place on a street named after a tree
- a street named after a tree
- yeah. a street named after a fucking tree

and he's narked for some reason. dead fucking narked but still fucking smiling.

- you up for it he says
- i suppose i say

the place is on kastanien allee. takes us just a mo to walk there. it's a bar. it's up some stairs and as we enter some shirtless auld leather queen says something. he reads bill's face and laughs.

- welcome to our queer home honey the queen says

yet another crappy american-kraut accent.

thom's already there. he hugs me but not bill.

i ask what kastanien means.

kastanien = chestnut.

- fucking told you bill says. a street named after a fucking tree

the place is scruffy and comfy but too public. we hear

kraut and british and aussie and american accents. others too. italian or spanish or something else maybe.

- gotta go score something bill says

he goes outside somewhere. it's his thing. what he's best at. doesn't know a soul and can't speak a word of kraut but he can score stuff. how the fuck does that work.

i stay with thom. thom buys the beers. at the counter he talks to some cute blonde guy. the blonde goes and thom turns to me.

- just a fuck buddy he says

like i give a toss.

we sit and drink the beers. we don't say much. and when bill returns we show thom the flyer for the underwear party. he knows the place where it's gonna be.

and on shaun-how-sir-alley we walk to the station then catch the funny yellow train. it's supposed to be the u-bahn. the underground. but it runs above the street.

we can't be arsed buying tickets. and there're no barriers anyway. we just walk on and off the trains.

- if we get caught there is a fine thom says
- whatever bill says

we change at alexanderplatz.

bill says he scored 6 tabs. 2 tabs for each of us. he's not sure what they are though. he thinks they might be acid.

- they called it trip. what else would it be

and on the way to the platform he swallows his 2 tabs then on the next train we pass graffiti on a wall. bill

Alone with the Germans

reads it out.

- sex and drugs and rock and roll he says

but that's not what's sprayed on the wall. sex and drugs and techno. that's what's on the wall. and i look at thom and thom looks at me. and we smile at each other. and then i take my 2 tabs. and thom reminds me about last night.

- after sisyphos you cried he says. you were fucked up
- sisyphos that the name of the club bill says. sissyfucks is better. i can fucking remember that

he laughs then he looks at me.

- he's just a fucking chippy he says

and to prove he ain't a chippy thom takes the tabs.

turns out that you do wear your shoes at an underwear party. if you want to. we keep our trainers on. some guys wear boots but boots and pants look wrong. there're lockers for your clothes. 6 euros entry. you get a numbered white plastic disc for the locker. an assistant has the key. the disc is on a rubber band. you use the disc to order drinks too. you pay when you leave. there's a drinks minimum of 6 euros per person. robbing bastards.

- what happens if you lose your disc bill says
- dunno i say

thom says nothing. i catch him looking at me.

there are 4 rooms in the place. a changing area with benches where we strip off. a room where there's a bar.

30

a dance floor. and a darkroom. red walls 'round the dance floor. black everywhere else. bill looks for the dj. his bare arse disappears into the crowd of men.

thom's pants are calvin klein too. white not black. the waistband is blue. the words calvin klein in white against the blue. i look at him and he smiles. i smile too. then bill returns.

- sounds like they're playing wax don't it he says. but there's no fucking dj

he goes on about it.

- there's no fucking dj. there should be a fucking dj but there's no fucking dj

then we get beers. then we dance. and it's horny. men in pants. young bodies. firm arses. flat bellies. pecs. biceps. definition without bulk. *schlanke männer*. bare skin. fresh sweat. nearness. bill and thom and me. we dance. we stomp. we hop. we turn. we bounce. we sweat.

and then thom takes my hand. he leads me away. away from the dance floor. away from bill. away from the other men.

and then i'm in the darkness.

i'm in the darkness with thom.

i'm in the darkroom with thom.

we can still hear the music and i can feel the bass through the walls. and some diva sings about true love. we hold each other and thom's skin is soft and warm.

- you should not call me a kraut he says. i heard you last night. it is disrespectful

31

Alone with the Germans

- i'm sorry i say. i'm really sorry. okay
- okay he says. please never say it again
- okay. i won't

and i mean it. i won't. and he believes me. and he smiles and we kiss and i touch him.

- what's this *auf deutsch* i say
- *mein arsch* he says

and i laugh and move my hand.

- and these
- *eier* he says

we say balls and they say eggs.

- and this

and we say cock and they say *schwanz* which means tail which doesn't make sense.

and we say belly and they say *bauch*.

and we say ears and they say *ohren.*

and we say lips and they say *lippen*.

and we say sex and they say *sex* but i don't wanna fuck. not there

- just hold me eh i say

and thom holds me and i think things.

i think that thom's better than bill who smiles all the time no matter what and won't ever let me fuck him.

i think i like being in the darkness with thom. i think i like thom. i think i like him a lot. and i wanna stay in the darkness with him but then it's the end of the night. and the lights come on.

then back on the dance floor bill's smiling and sweat-wet

and wasted and wearing someone else's t-shirt.

- i found the dj he says. he's up there

and he points up to a window above the dance floor. a bearded guy waves back at him.

- look he says. this t-shirt. he gave it to me
- oh yeah i say. and what did you give him

and he just smiles.

- look he says

and he pulls the front of the t-shirt up over his head and on the inside there's a picture. it's a face. a demon or a gargoyle or something. it's weird. bill's body with a gargoyle's face.

- *raus raus* the guy from the hostel shouts

he bangs at the door. he tries to open it but can't 'cause we locked it with the bolt. i become aware of other things. i'm hot. i'm sweating. i'm thirsty. i'm fully clothed. i'm in the middle. bill's behind me. thom's in front. it's light. it's bright. there're red numbers on the clock. it's 14:06. the guy from the hostel switches to english.

- check-out was at noon assholes

then he goes and i think how they'll charge an extra day on my credit card. then i fall back asleep. and when i wake up again it's 14:44. so i wake thom and bill. and we pack our cases. and i think that the flight from schönefeld might be at 16:35. bill has no fucking idea. and we can't find our boarding passes to check. and so

33

Alone with the Germans

thom checks on his iphone. and i'm right. we have less than two hours to catch the plane home. and we sneak out past reception. and then it happens.

it happens suddenly.

it happens on shaun-how-sir-alley.

bill can't keep up with us and thom looks at me.

- i want you to stay he says
- bill and me
- *nein* he says

bill catches up. he looks at thom then he looks at me.

- what's wrong he says

and i think about bill. about his smile. about the gargoyle face. and i think about home and mum and work. and i think about money. and i'm not stupid. not really. but i think about thom. about his skin. about calvin klein pants and about the diva singing. and i think about *eier* and *schwanz* and *ohren* and *lippen*. and none of that should matter should it. but there on shaun-how-sir-alley it does matter. it just fucking does.

Thorsten

Thorsten

Sean's iPod contained one thousand seven hundred and thirty-six tracks. Yet, he spent the flight repeatedly listening to just a handful of songs by Madonna. He needed to make a choice, to select a single song. It was important. Even so, after a while, his mind wandered and he recalled that in the Nineties certain gay magazines obsessed about which diva, Madonna or Kylie Minogue, commanded the largest gay male fan-base. For some reason, he recollected that the same magazines featured quizzes aimed at measuring the reader's compatibility with an object of his affection/lust/love. Sean was never exactly sure whether the quizzes were intended as a joke or not, but on occasion he completed them anyway.

The quizzes involved the reader making choices between a series of binaries. He was supposed to compare the quiz results with those of the object of his affection/lust/love. Yet, it was never entirely clear to Sean whether the other man should actually complete the quiz himself or if the reader should simply guess what he would choose. In any case, Sean knew that Brian would never take part. Sean would always opt for cooking with gas and not electricity and wearing briefs not boxer shorts. There was always a Kylie/Madonna binary, and he would obviously choose 'Madge' over 'La Minogue'. According to the quizzes, Brian and Sean were unsuited; Brian being a boxer shorts-wearing, Madonna-hater who cooked with electricity. Yet, despite what the quizzes indicated, Brian and Sean had been together for twenty-two years. Sean had never completed a quiz with Thorsten in mind, but the outcome would have been the same - incompatibility.

The quizzes were hokum, of course. There was no science involved. So why had Sean bothered completing them at all? Perhaps he simply had too much time on his hands. He had been young too (well, in his thirties) and that definitely had something to do with it. It was daft really! Yet, what was truly daft was that he should have ever thought about Thorsten in similar terms to Brian at all. And now! Well, he was on the flight.

'Why am I doing this?' he asked himself unwittingly turning the thought into words. The question was rhetorical; he knew exactly why he was on the flight. It was just that it had not been an easy decision to make and he still harboured doubts. As he sat listening to Madonna, he would have gone over everything in his mind one more time, but an electronic ping and the illumination of the seatbelt sign ended his musings. A steward then requested that Sean turn off his iPod and remove the earphones. Sean duly killed *Papa Don't Preach* and prepared for landing. The head steward broadcast a well-rehearsed spiel and the rest of the cabin crew checked passenger seatbelts then took their places.

As the plane descended, Sean looked out of the window. It was morning, but overcast. On the ground, he made out grey buildings and a patchwork of dirty greens and browns. Then, in the distance, he caught sight of it; the Great Needle, the *Fernsehturm*. It could be nowhere else. He was back! An emotion, amorphous and hard to restrain, welled up inside him. 'Oh, God!' he exclaimed.

It had been twenty-seven years. Back then, of course, the geography and the politics were different. He had been in West Berlin, an occupied city surrounded by the Wall. West Berlin and East Germany, were now long gone. He had flown British Airways and not Easyjet. The airport had been Tegel and not Schönefeld. The currency had been the Deutsch Mark and not the Euro. Sean had been twenty-five and not fifty-two.

As he peered out into the gloom, the aerial atop the *Fernsehturm* appeared to pierce the over-loaded grey nimbus that shrouded the city in gloom and the rain began.

He travelled light, nothing in the hold and a single item in the overhead locker (Brian's pull-along, borrowed without permission). There would be no need to wait at the carousel. On the way to passport control though, he had to stop several times to catch his breath and then the pain flared up. He winced and took two painkillers.

Alone with the Germans

He sat on a bench taking deep breaths until they kicked-in. As usual, the pills left him feeling giddy. A sensation that Sean suddenly realised was not too dissimilar to the wooziness that he used to feel after smoking the thin joints that Thorsten used to roll. And he pictured the German sitting crossed-legged assembling the joints on the cover of an old Udo Jürgens LP that he would rest on his lap.

Then, as Sean stood up and resumed the walk along the endless corridors, he noticed posters bearing the image of Franz Kafka, Thorsten's favourite author. They hung at regular intervals and advertised an exhibition at the *Literaturhaus*. In other circumstances, he might have added the exhibition to his itinerary. It was a bittersweet notion immediately countered by the unexpected feeling that even before reaching the city, Thorsten's presence had already touched him.

He negotiated passport control then ambled through the arrivals gate. Outside, at the taxi rank, the wind and rain pounded against him, but he quickly reached the front of the queue. A taxi pulled up and the driver climbed out. Blank-faced, he took the pull-along and placed it in the boot of his vehicle. Sean noted that he was tall, slim and red-haired. Middle-aged with a long face, green eyes and a narrow chin, he resembled Kafka as depicted in the *Literaturhaus* posters. The driver grunted something.

'Gleimstraße, *bitte*,' Sean answered.

Thorsten

The two men climbed into the taxi. Sean took the rear seat. As the taxi pulled away, the driver peered at Sean in the overhead mirror. '*Urlaub?*' he asked.

The question threw Sean. He had not expected to have to explain himself to anyone. A panic briefly took hold of him. He sat up from the slouch that he had adopted. 'No, I'm... I'm visiting someone,' he said before he attempted German. '*Ich besuche einen Freund. Verstehen?*'

The driver nodded then turned the radio on. The rain obscured the city from Sean's view. The windscreen wipers squeaked a counter-rhythm to the crass hip-hop that emanated from the cab's tiny, concealed speakers.

Sean wondered about Brian, whether he had found the note. If he had, he would have worried, of course. Brian worried at the best of times. And now, of course, he had something to worry about. Sean had left his iPhone (fully charged, switched on and not set to silent) at home in the bedroom. For the trip, he had bought a pay-as-you-go handset. Devious, but Sean could imagine the number of messages from Brian if he had brought the iPhone with him. Still, all his music was on the iPhone and he could not face flying without music, so he dug out and charged-up his old iPod.

Yet, whenever Brian found the note, Sean knew that he would inform the others and that they would all be on the case, but... Well, fuck them! Not that he meant them any ill will. It was just the situation – the constant fuss,

41

the relentless concern.

'I'm sorry, there's no cure,' Dr Sheikh, the specialist, had said. 'It's terminal.'

Yeah, well so was the pity! And do you know what? He did not want a cure. He did not want the surgery or the radiology or the chemotherapy or the medication or the blood transfusions. He did not want to lose what was left of his hair. He did not want more pills and scans and tests. He did not want everyone pulling together. He did not want anyone to care for him or devote effort to keeping him alive. He did not want to go through everything in the hope that it would buy him extra time. Time for what? He had lived a full life. He was loved and had loved. He had seen the world or, at least, something of it. He had lived well. Mostly, it had been a nice life. A nice life! God! That was part of it too, wasn't it? Oddly, perhaps, despite his health, too much of his life had been safe and secure. Something was missing and that something had seemed to be missing ever since West Berlin. What was it that Thorsten reckoned? '*Nett ist die kleine Schwester von Scheisse.*' Was that it? Nice is the little sister of shitty! Nice is actually worse than bad.

None of them would understand that. Certainly not Brian, who Sean recalled talking to Dr Sheikh after the diagnosis. 'I'll look after him. I know him better than anyone,' Brian had said. 'We're life partners.' True, but Sean had a life before Brian, a life about which Brian had never really enquired. That was the thing with Brian, he had a way of blocking out anything or anyone that he saw as a threat. He would just not talk about them in the hope that denial would diminish or erase the threat altogether. Strangely, it was only in that taxi as it sped along the motorway that Sean realised the true danger that Thorsten had always posed to Brian. Sean was in Berlin, of course, so Brian was right to fear him.

Still, Sean had wanted to involve Brian in his decision, but how could he? And not just because of Thorsten, although that was a big enough obstacle. Brian would never have agreed to help him, Sean was sure of that. And even if he had, Sean would have put Brian at risk of a criminal charge and prison. How could he do that? Better to do what he had to do alone.

And after it was all over, Sean was sure that Brian would follow his last wishes even though they were a work in progress. His plan had been to write them up before he came to Berlin and unobtrusively place a copy with his will in the filing cabinet. The plan failed, because Sean could not decide various matters (not just which Madonna song to play). In Berlin, Sean would have to make up his mind on the outstanding items then email his intentions to Brian. It felt messy, of course, but it was not a major problem.

Sheila, his sister, was potentially a far bigger difficulty; if she took control, selecting music or anything else would be pointless. She would choose two hymns then have some officiant read something dull from *The*

Bible. It had been from 'The Letter of St Paul to the Romans' for both Mum and Dad, why not make it a hat trick? And there would be some bland statements that said nothing meaningful about Sean or his life. Sheila had a knack for that, erasing the personal – Dad's obsession with his army days and punctuality, Mum's lifelong devotion to Mills and Boon and her compulsion for feeding wild birds. What would Sheila erase from his life - perhaps the fact that he was gay (or as she continued to say, 'homosexual')?

Yet, how could Sheila sidestep Brian? Didn't a partner trump a sibling in these matters? Brian would say that Sean had chosen how things were to be and that there was a moral argument, which she could not ignore. Sheila would doubtless claim that Sean was mentally ill - why else do what he had done? They would argue, but Sean hoped that Brian was up to the task of deflecting Sheila's intrusions. She was a control freak and obsessed about what people thought about her and the family – she had even pleaded with Sean not to come out, because it would upset Mum and Dad. Yet, it had hardly bothered them. Sheila was the one with the issue. Even so, Sean found that he could not hate her, not really. Family, eh?

As the taxi neared Alexanderplatz, the rain lightened and Sean thought that it might stop, but several minutes later, it was still raining when the cab turned on to

Thorsten

Gleimstraße. The taxi pulled-up outside the hotel. 'Can I hire you for the rest of today and tomorrow?' Sean asked. '*Verstehen Sie*?'

The driver's face crumpled. '*Als Stadtführer*?' he asked, which drew a blank expression from Sean. 'You are wishing me to show you the city?'

'No, that's not it,' Sean replied.

'*Als Chauffeur!*' Niels said. 'There is no need. I give my *Handynummer*. If I am free, I come. If not, Berlin has many taxis. Understand?'

Sean nodded.

'*Meine Name ist* Niels.'

'*Ich heiße* Sean.'

Niels carried the pull-along to the front step of the hotel where Sean paid him. Niels then presented Sean with a business card. '*Meine Handynummer,*' he said pointing at a mobile phone number scrawled below the taxi company's logo.

Neat and clean and modern, but tiny; the room barely provided space to stand. It reeked of air-freshener. *Ersatz* roses, Sean thought. It was on the ground floor as requested, but at the back of the building, overlooking a small, dreary courtyard. In normal circumstances, he would have complained, but as it was, he did not see the point. He unpacked then showered. He dressed then sat on the bed and felt what? Lost? Angry? Confused? Alone? All of those things? None of those things? He was not

45

sure. He had no sense of his whereabouts in the city. He was in the east, but had in any case, only ever briefly visited the west and so long ago that it was bound to have changed in innumerable ways. And he knew no one except Niels, which hardly counted at all.

As well as doubt and fear though, he experienced something of the exhilaration that he had felt on the first afternoon of that first visit. When he stayed at a hotel near the *Zooligischer Garten* and wandered along the Ku'damm, the main drag, and found the *Europa Zentrum* with its hoardings advertising a cabaret featuring topless female dancers. And when, despite his limited German, he nervously ordered a beer in a nearby bar. '*Ein kleines Glas Bier bitte.*'

And the waiter says, 'Very good! You understand German adjective endings.' And Sean feels proud. (Yet, in hindsight, he thought the remark patronising, mocking).

And then there was that first evening, when he takes the U-Bahn to Nollendorfplatz and wanders around Schöneberg with a *Spartacus Gay Guide* in his jacket pocket and West Berlin seems alien, dangerous and therefore exciting, electric. A city unlike any other city that he has visited. A capitalist island in a communist sea. An outpost. A frontier town.

And the twenty-five-year-old Sean is consumed with a wild and aching openness for an adventure, a need to meet someone – a man, but a man different from the others that he has known or, more precisely, half-known. A man unlike any Englishman. A foreign man. A German man with a deep voice who rolled his *R*s. A man that had a name like Hartmut or Lüder or Jürgen.

Yes, that first night, when like Christopher Isherwood, the writer that Sean so admired, he is on his own, alone in Berlin. An Englishman alone with the Germans.

Outside, the rain stopped. Sean had assumed that the weather would delay his activities, but he suddenly found himself unsure what to do. He sighed then stood up. 'I should eat,' he thought. He pulled his coat on and then on Gleimstraße he absent-mindedly headed away from the main drag. As he walked, he noticed a dreary, pockmarked facade amongst the fine-fronted apartment buildings. He recalled Thorsten, an *Ossi* - an East German, telling him that even in the Eighties many buildings in the East were still 'war wounded'.

And Sean recalled the rest of that conversation, reliving it in his head as the German says, 'I was in prison for six months.' And his younger self gasps, while questions run through his head. What was Thorsten's crime - political, sexual, drug-related? And how long was the sentence? Sean does not like to ask though. And then, in a hoarse growl, Thorsten reveals that he has lived in West Berlin for three years. 'Honecker, our beloved leader,' he says, 'no longer wanted me.' He takes a deep breath. '*Ich vermisse meine Mutti.*' And

Alone with the Germans

young Sean thinks of how, in the same circumstances, he would have missed his own mother.

They stand side by side, shirtless in the summer heat, at the open window of the apartment in the dilapidated block on the scruffy Kreuzberg street that Thorsten squats with his friend Wolfgang. 'Look at it!' Thorsten moans. '*Scheisse!* No one wants to live here, surrounded on these three sides by *die Mauer*. So we took it over.'

And Sean is unsure who 'we' actually are, gay men or some political faction. And the two men look toward the Wall, which seems insignificant, distant, a narrow grey, graffiti-covered ribbon visible beyond the gap between other neglected buildings. Behind it, nothing, just grey and haze, summer heat rising up off the death strip.

'*Bist du glücklich*?'

'Am I happy?' Sean replies. 'Of course. You?'

'*Ja, ich auch,*' Thorsten says and sucks on the joint.

Even then, without knowing what was to come, Sean doubted that Thorsten was happy. Beautiful Thorsten with his flat, hard stomach and perfect legs. Thorsten who talked of *Selbstfinden* - of finding himself in West Berlin and writers, Isherwood and the Manns – Thomas and his son Klaus, but most of all Franz Kafka whose tale, 'Metamorphosis', obsessed and amused him. An obsession that, in hindsight, at least, seemed to signify something dark and foreboding as, perhaps, did Thorsten's musical tastes – Second Decay, DAF, Einstürzende Neubauten, Lou Reed. Wasn't there

48

something dark and Kafkaesque in that music too? Yet, what about Nina Hagen, the punk, an *Ossi* like Thorsten? Nina his muse, his *Prinzessin*, his Madonna. Nina Hagen - fun, crazy, outlandish. She was not Kafkaesque, surely?

And as Sean traipsed along Gleimstraße, he recalled another scene; Thorsten playing a Nina Hagen album on a turntable on the exposed floorboards of the living room. The album cover with an image of Nina smoking a cigarette is propped against the bare-plastered wall. The music is loud and Sean sits in his underwear on a pile of beanbags and pillows laughing while Thorsten dances before him, topless with his jeans unbuttoned. Suddenly, Wolfgang - naked, tall, muscular with dark curly hair, storms in from his bedroom. Angry and demanding, the Bavarian shocks Sean with the volume of his voice and the rage that distorts his face, but most of all, Sean is jolted by Wolfgang's unabashed nakedness. Thorsten just laughs. He stops dancing, bends down and reduces the volume of the music. He placates his flatmate, 'Wolfi' he calls him. He hugs him, pats him on the bare buttock. *'Jetzt kannst du schlafen,'* he says, and as he holds Wolfgang, he winks at young Sean who sits rigid, unsure and confused by the physical closeness of the two Germans. He thought them just friends, but was there more to it?

Further along Gleimstraße, Sean started out from his recollections to find that he had followed some people onto an area of rough, broken ground surrounded by shrubs and trees. A sign indicated that he had entered Mauerpark. In the distance, across an expanse of flat, muddy grass, he saw a congregation of people and long, snaking rows of tarpaulin-covered stalls. Without thinking, he headed toward them.

He was out of breath when he reached the nearest stall. He stood for a while to catch his breath then walked along looking at the usual flea market shit - t-shirts, kitsch, second hand clothes, books, bric-a-brac and local crafts as well as fake and/or over-priced Soviet and DDR memorabilia. Nothing interested him, but he nonetheless wandered along looking for God knows what. How did it have anything to do with Thorsten?

At a second-hand music stall, he looked through the racks and found a Nina Hagen CD. He scanned the track listing. One track stood out; *Born to Die in Berlin.* He laughed. He bought the CD. Eight Euros. A rip off, but he did not haggle. He wandered around for a further twenty minutes before he bought a *Bratwurst* and roll from another stall. He sat eating it and drinking filter coffee in a covered area, where he and others sheltered from another downpour.

Some minutes later, the rain subsided and he continued to wander about the park. He came to the Max Schmeling Halle, a huge arena, the name of which seemed vaguely familiar. For some reason, Sean wondered whether Madonna had ever played there, a thought that coincided with a sharp stab of pain on the left side of his abdomen. He had to sit on a bench to catch his breath and take more painkillers. After a while, the pain subsided and on the same bench, a young woman with red hair looked at him. 'Are you okay?' She had a strong German accent.

Sean wondered how she knew that he was English. 'I'm fine,' he lied.

'Madonna played here a few years ago,' she said. 'Quite a show, I am believing.'

Spooked, he immediately got up and walked back to Gleimstraße, where he phoned Niels, who collected him a few minutes later.

'*Wo gehen wir*?' Niels asked.

'*Brandenburger Tor, bitte*,' Sean replied.

At home, Sean had a black and white photograph of himself standing in front of the Wall at the back of the *Brandenburger Tor*, which had then been located on the East German side of the barrier. He kept the photograph in an album with snaps of his parents. In the photograph, he stares directly at the camera. He wears a black nylon jacket, faded jeans, a black t-shirt and black Doctor Marten's – shoes not boots. He stands in front of a warning sign; *ACHTUNG! SIE VERLASSEN JETZT WEST BERLIN*.

On the day that Thorsten took the photograph, the sky was clear and there was virtually no one else around.

Alone with the Germans

Twenty-seven years later, the cloud was low and grey and there were thousands of tourists. Sean weaved in and out of the crowds in an attempt to find the spot where he had stood in the photograph. He recalled Thorsten stooping down to take the shot with his single lens reflex camera. The brand - Praktica, is East German as is the Carl Zeiss wide-angle lens. Thorsten is oddly patriotic about the fact. 'My cousin works at the Carl Zeiss laboratory,' he gushes. 'They produce only quality products.' Thorsten then spends some time preparing for the shot, checking the direction of the sun to make sure that Sean is not squinting and ensuring that the background is uncluttered. Then, when he has positioned Sean, he shouts, 'Your hair!' Sean is uncertain what he means, but rakes his fingers across the top of his head. '*Geil!*' Thorsten shouts and clicks the shutter.

Amongst the tourists, Sean had no idea where he had stood when Thorsten took the photograph. After fifteen minutes, he gave up and although Thorsten – anti-capitalist and anti-American - would have disapproved, Sean had *Kaffee und Kuchen* at the nearby Starbucks.

That evening, Sean picked at the lamb tagine and couscous he had ordered at a restaurant on Schönhauser Allee, the main drag near his hotel. Afterwards, he was the only customer in a bar. He sat with a glass of *Hock* and watched the world pass-by; couples holding hands, groups of young people, people walking dogs, cyclists, cars, buses and trams as well as the yellow trains that shuttled along the overhead railway. The cloud and rain had gone. He loved it all - the fruitiness of the wine, the clear evening, the people, the traffic, the buildings and the wide avenue in front of him. 'The world will go on without me,' he thought. Was he resentful? He thought not, but then the deep, sharp pain that he had come to know so well returned. He gasped and clutched at his side. The pain was nearly always on the left despite the cancer having spread throughout his body.

After the bar, he had intended to call Niels and go to Kreuzberg or Schöneberg, but it was not to be. Exhausted from travel and woozy from more painkillers, he spent the night at the hotel.

At 5:17, he woke suddenly. It happened often enough. The usual causes (headache, discomfort, coughing, itchiness, nausea, vomiting, cramp or diarrhoea) had more to do with the medication than the cancer, but were all absent. The green LED display on the radio-alarm clock glowed on the bedside table next to him. Looking up at the white, flat ceiling, he began to think about the day, where he would go, Schöneberg then Kreuzberg - in that order, and what he would do when he got there, which seemed less certain.

Then he realised what had woken him; it had been a dream. He could not remember the dream, but there was a residue, a vague sense of something. And as he thought about it, he grew aware of what that something was. If he had been a person of faith, he might have considered the dream a message from God. Even so, there was something like religion behind his realisation that the dream concerned Thorsten. He knew it. And as he lay looking at the ceiling, he recalled Thorsten's eyes, blue and wide, and the way he drew his lips into a smile to show his uneven, white teeth, and the slight whistling sound he sometimes made when he drew on a joint.

Smiling, Sean drifted back to sleep until seven o'clock, when he climbed out of bed and showered then dressed and took his meds. He breakfasted on coffee and a croissant at a bakery opposite the hotel.

A mild autumn morning, the sky was a pale, watery blue and the cool, low sun was powerful enough to dazzle. Residents and tourists began to fill the pavements and the cafes. Trains and trams and other traffic sped along Schönhauser Allee, where, a little later, he bought a postcard and a stamp from a gift shop. The postcard bore the words 'Nach Regen kommt Sonne' above a triptych of simple graphic images – cloud and rain on the left, a rainbow in the centre and the sun on the right. He sat at a table in the bakery where he had breakfast and ordered a coffee. He addressed the card to Brian then pondered what to write. He sighed and sniffed, but did not cry. He could not come up with anything – 'Sorry, I love you' was just inadequate. He gave up the exercise, took out his mobile phone and called Niels who collected him a few minutes later for the drive to Schöneberg.

The plan was that Niels would drop Sean at Nollendorfstraße, but there had been a major accident. After sitting in gridlocked traffic for twenty minutes, Niels suggested that Sean should walk. 'It is just some minutes that way,' he said pointing down Uhlandstraße. Sean climbed out of the taxi and followed Niels's directions, but as he got to a vacant shop front there was something about the shape of the door and the size and position of the windows that attracted his attention. Once, it had been a men's boutique. And with that realisation, Sean encountered his younger self exiting the door, carrying a plastic carrier bag that his older self knew to contain a t-shirt bearing the slogan *Der Tot ist ein Dandy*, the title of an Einstürzende Neubaten song. His younger self is a looker, slim, well-proportioned, with a decent face and cute white-toothed smile. His dark hair is shaved at the back and sides, but longer on top. The body of his older self had deteriorated, of course, middle-age spread followed by weight loss and the ravages of medication and chemo- and radiotherapy, which had greyed and thinned his hair. Still, his old brown eyes were like his young brown eyes, warm and kind, only a little duller. Both Seans were unshaven, stubbly. Young Sean wears the Doc Martens, jeans, a thick studded leather belt and a white short-sleeved t-shirt with a red panel advertising *The Man Machine,* the Seventies Kraftwerk album. He saunters off in the direction of Nollendorfplatz. His older self looked through the neglected facade to the boutique that had once housed a window display comprising a series of the same black and white picture of a naked male torso above the words, *'Jeans, Mode, Trends'.*

Sean wandered around Schönefeld for an hour. He recognised nothing except the U-Bahn station, but then, he found Tom's Bar and observed his younger self with Thorsten, drunk and elated in the early hours. His younger self wears the *Der Tot ist ein Dandy* t-shirt and the Doc Martens with dark jeans. Thorsten, taller and broader than the young Englishman, wears heavy black boots, a white long-sleeved t-shirt and faded jeans. His short light-brown hair is gelled back. For a moment, the older Sean desperately looked around for the club where they had first met and danced together, but had no idea of the name or location of the place.

He then watched as Thorsten kisses his younger self. A drunken, imprecise kiss, the older Englishman stroked his face feeling the wire-like stumble of the German's cheek against the younger Englishman's skin. He smiled and his heart beat as fiercely as it does for young Sean.

'Come on then,' Thorsten says when they unhitch and leads the young Sean by the hand.

'Where are we going?'

Thorsten

'*Ich wohne in* Kreuzberg *dreiunddreissig.*' Kreuzberg 36 means nothing to young Sean and Thorsten explains about the *Postleitzahl* - the postcode; 36 is the most radical, queerest district of West Berlin.

They walk some distance, chatting and passing a cigarette back and forth between themselves, then enter a path at the side of a canal. 'What do you do?' Sean asks.

Thorsten pulls a business card from his pocket. Sean takes it and notes the motif of footsteps and arrows and the strapline, *Die Tanzschule für Sie.*

'You're a dance teacher!' Sean exclaims.

Thorsten laughs and grabs hold of Sean. He takes the lead, waltzes him around then dips him tango-style, but they collapse on to the ground. They laugh and Sean sniffs up, he can smell something. '*Etwas riecht!*'

Thorsten gets it too. 'It does not smell,' he says. '*Es stinkt.*' They laugh. Some of the dog shit from the path is on Thorsten's jeans. 'Oh, no,' he squeals, 'I got do-do on my tutu.' And the two men cannot stop guffawing for a long while. Then Thorsten wipes his jeans with a handkerchief that he discards in a trashcan. 'And so,' he announces dramatically, 'the myth of perfect German public hygiene is revealed as a lie.'

They hold hands and further along the path at a streetlight, Thorsten stops. He looks at the canal. 'What is it?' Sean asks.

'Something has broken the surface of the water.'

Alone with the Germans

'Are there fish? It looks foul.'

'I do not think so,' Thorsten says then tells Sean about the stream, a tributary of the River Saale, which flows through his hometown and how, when he was a boy, he was with his father and they had seen a large fish jump out of the water. And his father had told him that it was the lonely, old *Carfenfisch*, the last of its kind in the stream. It cried constantly, but because it lived in water, no one ever saw its tears.

'How sad,' Sean says and kisses Thorsten on the cheek. They stare at each other for a moment, before Thorsten ends the seriousness with a smile.

The sun had begun its descent when Niels dropped Sean in Kreuzberg near the U-Bahn station on Mehringdamm. At Mustafa's *Gemüse Kebap* stall, a long queue snaked along the crowded pavement. The traffic was noisy and pop music blared out from a cafe. The street smelt of chilli and roasted vegetables from the stall and petrol from the traffic, but it was harder to identify the origins of a sweet chemical odour that hung in the air around the U-Bahn entrance.

Like Schöneberg, at first, nothing in Kreuzberg was familiar, but then Sean walked to the crossroad with Yorckstraße and he recognised the twin spires of Sankt Bonafatius church. In the crowd, he immediately encountered Thorsten and his younger self with Wolfi and Ahmed, Wolfi's Moroccan boyfriend. He knew that the

58

young men were going to a club, Schwuz, somewhere on the Mehringdamm. Yet, he had no interest in the location of Schwuz. Instead, he tried to make out the direction that the men came from, because that might have indicated where the squat had been located. Tired, disorientated by the crowds and disheartened by his experiences in Schöneberg and at the *Brandenburger Tor*, it was bound to be a challenge. Even so, Sean attempted it.

Yet, as he trod the pavement, he recalled the evening with Thorsten after the events on the canal. How they hail a cab and sit on the rear seat holding hands and chatting while the driver watches them in the overhead mirror. And how they arrive at the squat where Sean pays the driver. And then, after Thorsten fumbles to open the entrance door, they dash up the stairs. And inside the squat, the smell of sweat, mould and cannabis and the sight of bare walls and floorboards appals Sean. The furniture is old and gnarled and the collection of pillows and beanbags that act as a sofa are stained. Yet, after a moment, Thorsten hands him a bottle of beer and Sean gets over himself.

And in the living room, on the pillows and beanbags, they drink and smoke some joints. Thorsten plays eerie electronic music on the turntable and they talk. They talk for hours. They talk about film and literature and music. About Brad Davis, Sean's favourite actor who played Billy in *Midnight Express* and the sailor in *Querelle*, the film based on a Genet novel. About Derek Jarman, whose film *Caravaggio* Thorsten thought a brilliant depiction of queer passion. About the Manns, Thomas and his son Klaus, both of whom appealed to the Englishman and the German. About Franz Kafka too, of course, but mainly '*Verwandlung*', the short story that Thorsten thought incorrectly translated into English as 'Metamorphosis'.

'That title,' he says, 'suggests the biological change in insects, but in the story, the change in the character has nothing to do with biology.'

And they talk about music. About Joy Division and New Order and Iggy Pop and Lou Reed and David Bowie and Kraftwerk and the *Neue Deutsche Welle*. Yet, they mainly talk about Nina Hagen who Thorsten adored for what seemed to Sean to be reasons to do with a shared East German background rather than anything else.

And later, on the mattress on the floor in the bedroom they strip and kiss and grope each other before Thorsten pushes himself into Sean. Afterwards, sleepy and loving, Thorsten strokes Sean's face. '*Wir haben gelebt, geliebt und gelernt,*' he says. 'Understand?'

'We have lived, loved and learnt?'

Thorsten nods then utters a single word, '*Kuscheln.*' Sean complies, pulling the duvet about them and wrapping his arms around the German.

In the end, Sean walked the length of Yorckstraße and back, but the location of the squat remained a mystery.

Thorsten

Defeated, he gave up and returned to the Mehringdamm, where he took a seat in the window of Café Melita Sundstrum. On the next table, another customer, a middle-aged American man, sat with a young woman. 'This is the most famous gay cafe in Berlin,' he said.

The phrase resonated with Sean, because Thorsten had once talked about Cafe Anal, a place with huge, black dildos in the window and Tom of Finland prints on the walls. 'Next time you visit,' Thorsten says, 'we must go there. It is the most famous gay cafe in Berlin.'

A waiter approached Sean and he ordered *Milchkaffee*. And while he waited, he watched the people on the street; punks, hipsters, *Tunten,* businesspeople, tourists, Buddhists, police officers, beggars. And when his drink came, he recalled that he once had *Milchkaffee* with Thorsten at Movie, a cafe-cum-bar, which he thought might have been near a bridge in the district of Charlottenberg.

Movie has black and white framed photographs of movie stars – Marlene Dietrich, Marilyn Monroe and others, most of whom Sean does not recognise. There is a jukebox and someone selects a kitschy, crass love song sung by some obscure diva and the clientele, seven or eight young men, sing along. An awful song, but a camp song and the barman, a short fair-haired man in his thirties shouts that they are *Tunten*. Everyone laughs, but Sean does not know the word.

'You would say queens,' Thorsten explains before he

goes to the jukebox and to the displeasure of the other men, who moan and shout comments, selects a Nina Hagen song - a rock number sung in English.

And after Movie, Thorsten and Sean travel back to Kreuzberg to meet Wolfi and Ahmed and go to Schwuz where the music is mixed, erratic – Abba and DAF and Donna Summer and AC/DC and Einstürzende Neubauten and God knows what else. And the dancing is just as crazy, but no one cares.

And hours later, back at the squat, Sean is stoned, drunk, happy, but then he is alone with Wolfi and Ahmed who kiss him about the face. And he does not know where Thorsten is. And he loses it, shouting and screaming and pushing the two men away from him. And then Thorsten is there holding him, stroking his hair and saying something. *'Es wird okay sein.'* Is that what he says? Whatever it is, he says it over and over. *'Es wird okay sein. Es wird okay sein.'*

And really, that is the first time that Sean thinks that he is not alone, that there is someone for him.

And the next day, hungover and eating toast in bed, they talk about things. Wolfi and Ahmed meant no harm, but Sean was unaccustomed to such behaviour and, drunk and stoned, it freaked him out. 'We need to clear the air with them,' Sean says.

'We do,' Thorsten agrees.

And then the Englishman and the German discuss how, despite living in different countries, they can be a couple, an item. How Sean will go home, but return in a few months, when he has saved enough for the flight and living expenses for at least a few weeks. And how, in the meantime, they will keep in touch and Sean will take more German lessons not because he has to - Thorsten's English is good, but because he wants to. And how they can regularly talk on the telephone for free, because Wolfi is a telex operator at an American company and when he works nights, he is alone in the office and allows Thorsten to make calls.

That night, after returning from Kreuzberg to the hotel, Sean sat at his laptop and played the Nina Hagen CD that he had bought at the flea market. The song *Born to Die in Berlin* disappointed him on two levels. First, looking at the credits on the CD case, it was released in the Nineties so it could not have been the song that he had heard with Thorsten at Movie. Second, it was a ballad, which seemed to undermine his belief in Nina as fun, crazy, outlandish.

Yet, the song was credited to not only Nina Hagen, but Dee Dee Ramone. Sean googled the song title and found then listened to a Ramones version, which was - as expected, guitar-driven. He downloaded it, but also copied Nina's rendition from the CD. Then he updated his iPod with both songs before he opened a document on his laptop simply entitled 'Instructions'. He typed a few sentences then read over what he had written.

Alone with the Germans

Sean hoped that Brian would play the songs that he had selected - a beautiful, religious chant by the Hildegard von Bingen Choir, Madonna's *Live to Tell* and the Ramones version of *Born to Die in Berlin.* Thinking about it, he doubted that the Ramones song would actually get played at his funeral, but regardless, he copied the document into the body of an email and then pressed the send button.

He was about to shut down the laptop when he noticed the inbox. He sat and stared at the screen. He wanted to respond to Brian's email. He wanted to say thanks. To say sorry. To say look after yourself. To say I know it might not feel like it, but I do love you. Yet, he could say none of that. He simply could not. If he opened the email, there was a chance that he would not see things through. He could not let that happen. He simply couldn't. He pressed the power button and the laptop shut down.

And afterwards, he sat motionless and remembered the holidays in Tenerife and Portugal. And Hector, their long-dead Labrador. And the day Brian's father died and Brian had sobbed into Sean's shoulder. And their first meeting, that night at the Curzon after Sean had been dumped by that prick Kevin. And how Brian always liked to sleep nearest to the bedroom door. And how he always smelt of *Eau Sauvage* cologne. And how he liked his coffee strong, but his tea weak. And then Sean cried. He cried for a long while.

Thorsten

*

Later, he felt a huge sense of disappointment. Berlin had changed too much, he thought. West Berlin and East Germany were gone, of course, not only another era, but another country as they (whoever *they* are) say. To some degree, the many changes in the city might have accounted for the fact he had not found the squat, the club where he had met Thorsten or the spot where Thorsten took the photograph at *Brandenburger Tor*.

His disappointment also had to do with a failure of memory. He had forgotten so much - places, streets, buildings, events. He could not even remember the very first time he had laid eyes on Thorsten in that club in Schöneberg – though that possibly had much to do with the fact that he had been so drunk.

He had not been as methodical in his search for Thorsten as he could have been either. He did not go to all the places he should have. As well as the *Brandenburger Tor* and Schöneberg and Kreuzberg, Sean could have visited Charlottenburg, because Movie was (perhaps) located there. And also Tegel Airport, where they had a brief, emotional farewell.

Yet, what disappointed Sean the most was that he did not understand what it was about Thorsten that so beguiled him. What had brought him back after so many years? He had thought that he knew – or at least had some kind of a handle on it, but his insight seemed less solid than it had been just a few days before. What he had with Thorsten was special, he was sure of that. Why was it special though? And why was it more special than what he had with Brian? It was not first love – there had been others. Thorsten and Sean shared interests too – music and literature and film and whatever, but that wasn't it either. So was it something about the dance on the canal? Or the story about the crying fish? Or was it the fact that Thorsten had rescued him from Wolfi and Ahmed? Or was Thorsten really – even without the deep voice and rolling *R*s, that man, that German, that Sean had always wanted? He could not be certain, which, on some level, seemed to indicate that the whole venture was a mistake, a failure.

On the other hand, did it really matter what it was about Thorsten that beguiled him? It just did, no need to overanalyse things. Perhaps it was just as Thorsten had said, '*Wir haben gelebt, geliebt und gelernt.*' Yes, in the short time that they had been together, they had lived, loved and learnt. That was it surely, wasn't it?

'Pick me up from the hotel in five minutes,' Sean said when he phoned Niels for the last time. He then bundled most of his possessions into Brian's pull-along. He sat on the bed and pushed the painkillers and other pills out from their blister packs. He put them into a small plastic bag, which he placed in the left pocket of his overcoat. He unscrewed the top off a half bottle of brandy that he had bought earlier that day while he had waited for Niels to collect him from Kreuzberg. He took a long slug and squirmed as he swallowed the bitter, warming liquid. Then he screwed the cap back on to the bottle. He placed the bottle into the right pocket of his overcoat. He laid the pull-along on the bed and checked that the room was tidy. He ensured that his iPod, wallet, mobile phone and passport were in his inside pockets then he left the room.

Outside, there was a half moon, no clouds. The wind was light. Gleimstraße was quiet, hardly a soul about. After a few moments, Niels pulled up.

'*Zum* Tiergarten,' Sean commanded as he climbed into the front seat. '*Die Siegessäule,*' he added as he pulled the door shut.

During the journey, Niels glanced at Sean several times, but the Englishman appeared glum and distracted, continuously looking out of the window.

As agreed, Niels dropped Sean near the *Siegessäule* - the Victory Column, and then Sean paid the fare. Niels counted the notes. 'There is too much,' he said pushing several notes back at Sean.

'No, take it,' Sean commanded then surprised the German, leaning across and briefly hugging him. '*Danke,*' Sean said. '*Danke.*'

Niels reluctantly accepted the tip then Sean climbed out of the taxi and headed toward the tower.

After a moment, Niels realised something. 'You must be careful,' he shouted. 'Out here so late. You want that I wait?'

Alone with the Germans

Sean did not respond.

On a bench, Sean sits and stares up at the great golden angel at the tower's summit then he looks around. Somewhere in the trees, twenty-seven years previously, Thorsten had hung himself.

He takes the bag of pills from his overcoat pocket. He looks at it and begins to cry. 'Oh, God,' he sobs. 'Oh, God.' It takes a minute for the tears to stop and then he takes a deep breath. He swallows the pills. He washes each handful down with brandy. When the bag is empty, he exhales deeply. He sniffles then runs a hand across his nose and mouth. He takes the iPod from his inside pocket. He plugs the earphones into his ears. He selects a track. The Ramones version of *Born to Die in Berlin* blasts into his head.

And then Sean looks up to see Thorsten, as he knew that he would. They smile. Thorsten pulls Sean to his feet and takes one of the earphones and inserts it into his own ear. 'Let's dance,' he says, 'but not to this noisy trash.' Nina Hagen's growl immediately replaces Joey Ramones's drawl. They hold each other and sway to the music.

'I prefer the Ramones version,' Sean says.

'Well, you'll hear it at your funeral.'

'Will I?'

'Perhaps not, but if we're going to dance, Nina's version is better.'

Thorsten

'And how would you know?' Sean asks. 'You were dead before it was even released.'

Thorsten smiles, but says nothing.

After a moment, Sean's phone rings, startling him.

'It's your driver,' Thorsten explains. 'He worries for you.' He frowns. 'You could go back, you know? It is still not too late.'

Sean thinks about it. 'No,' he says shaking his head. 'There's no going back.' After another moment, the ringing dies. They sway and dance, Sean resting his head on the German's shoulder, before he looks up into Thorsten's face. 'Why did you do it?' he asks.

'Wolfi never told you?'

Sean shakes his head. 'He only said, '*Thorsten raucht nicht mehr*' and that they found you in the Tiergarten.'

The German laughs. 'Thorsten smokes no more! *Typisch Deutsch*!' He nuzzles into Sean. 'I got a diagnosis,' he says. 'You know what that meant back then.'

'But I was okay.'

'That's just the way the cookie crumbles.'

'I wanted to go to your funeral.'

'What can I say? My family...'

Sean nods then Thorsten pulls away and looks at him. 'What?' Sean asks.

'Pills are a bad idea, you know? You'll die a slow and painful death. Hanging is quicker, cleaner.'

'Maybe, but let's not think about it, eh?'

Alone with the Germans

'Okay,' Thorsten agrees. 'It is your death.'

Sean ends the seriousness with a smile. 'Did I ever ask what you prefer, boxer shorts or briefs?'

'*Verrückter Engländer!*' Thorsten says. 'You forget, I did not wear underwear.'

They laugh then dance until the song ends.

In the silence, they look at each other for one long, last moment.

'This is it, isn't it' Sean says.

Thorsten nods then utters a single word, '*Kuscheln.*' Sean complies, pulling his overcoat about them and wrapping his arms around the German.

Beans and Stew

Beans and Stew

I see him through my hotel window. As agreed, he's
waiting near the bus stop on Wilhelm-Külz-Straße. In his
black, short-sleeved t-shirt, jeans and boots, he's almost
a silhouette against the wall behind him. He's taller and
thinner than he appears in his profile photos, but I know
that it's him by the shape of his head and the thick,
close-cropped, dark hair. He has wide shoulders, big
arms, a proper waist, no beer belly. He keeps himself fit
– the standout line on his profile is, *'Ich bin ein so
sportlicher Typ.'* He's in good nick - for his age. From this
distance though, I can't see his face, and that's what I go
on, the face. The photos on his profile aren't clear either.
No close head and shoulder poses, just fuzzy, low
resolution, full figure shots; him standing in shorts and
vest on a beach and another in front of the sign for Loro
Parque Zoo. Holiday snaps. No nudes. The thing is, they
usually lie about their age. Well, most of them do, when
they reach forty or thereabouts. Understandable really, I
suppose. They put up old photos too. His photos could be
old, but his silhouette, at least, looks good.

On the other hand, he's ten minutes early. A bad sign.
It smacks of desperation. Too eager. I bet I'm the best

thing that's come his way in a while. I'm not being arrogant or bigheaded either; you only have to search the local profiles to see what I mean. I know that it's about who's online at any particular time and really, mornings are never the best time to go on the sniff, but besides his profile, I didn't see any worth a second look. Not one. Shocking really.

I move away from the window and sit on the edge of the bed, where I finish towelling myself dry. I briefly turn my interest to the television. *MDR aktuell*, the local news programme, streams live footage from a demonstration. I catch the odd word or phrase from the unseen, deep-voiced commentator, '*Neo-Nazis... Anti-Nazis... Gewalt.*' Then I concentrate on dressing, but as I pull my Levi's on, an image catches my attention. A tall, shaven-headed man, sneering and wearing a black bomber jacket extends his right hand. He raises it above his round head and shouts something. He pulls his arm back to repeat the salute, but there's an immediate, clumsy cut to a wide-angle view of the nationalist marchers.

I fasten my jeans then reach for the remote control. I press a button and the demonstration is gone. Then I'm out of the door and in the hallway. There's no one at reception and I disobey the rules, taking my room key with me.

On the street, it's breezy and there's a smell of garlic from the steakhouse on the corner. I can hear birdsong over the low drone of traffic. He is still leaning against the grey wall beyond the bus stop. He sees me exit the hotel and stands up straight. I head toward him.

He must have been a handsome youth. He's still a looker. He has a wide forehead, a big, prominent brow, a short wide nose, full lips and blue-grey eyes. Clean-shaven with a square jaw, he's going grey at the temples and there are lines at the corner of his eyes, but it looks good on him. His profile photos could be so much better.

He takes me in, raises his eyebrows, smiles. I stretch out a hand. '*Hallo*,' I say. 'I am John.'

He takes my hand. A firm grip. Warm, callused skin. '*Bin der Edgar*,' he growls.

By the time we reach the corner before the main square, several things are established. He's aware of the march by the nationalists and the demonstration against them, but he has no interest in either faction. He's fifty-one (though his profile indicates that he's forty-five). He's the office manager for the local branch of a large non-governmental organisation. He hates his job – too many personalities and too much politics, but the money is good. He was married, but his wife left him nine years ago – she's in Austria with a richer man. He likes me or, at least, the look of me.

'I am new to this,' he says.

'That's okay,' I say.

We look at each other for a few moments, but the

silence gets to him. 'I have a son,' he says, which perhaps proves his previous point. He opens his wallet and hands me a small photograph. 'He is named Matthias. He is twenty-nine years of age.'

'Three years younger than me,' I reply and he pulls a face, dropping the corners of his mouth and pouting. 'He looks like you,' I say and return the snap to him.

'Yes, he does,' Edgar agrees, slipping the picture back into his wallet. 'He is taller than me, over two metres big. He has taken on weight and....' He pauses, searching for the correct word perhaps, but then thinks better of it. He looks at me, holds my stare for a moment and raises his eyebrows. 'Something to eat?'

'Yes.'

'*Italienisch oder –*'

'*Thüringisch,*' I suggest.

'Ah, yes, when in Rome,' he smiles. 'I know a nice place.' Then, as we continue to the main square, we encounter an older woman, perhaps in her late sixties, walking a dachshund. The dog barks. Edgar frowns. She says something to him and he answers. They talk quickly and I don't catch a word. I stoop down to the dog. '*Wie hübsch,*' I say, looking up. '*Wie heißt er?*'

The woman gazes down at me. The dog sniffs my hand. 'Bert,' she says sternly then Edgar says something to her.

I pat Bert while Edgar and the woman converse. After a few moments, I stand up. Bert yaps at me then Edgar and the woman exchange farewells. We continue on our way. 'She is such a mouth,' Edgar growls. 'She will be telling everyone about you.'

'Is that a problem?'

'No,' he says. 'Not so much.' A few metres further along, we turn a corner and he glances at me again. 'The main square,' he announces. A hundred metres ahead, the high, severe spires of the Severin Kirche and the cathedral stab the sky.

'Lovely,' I say.

'Yes, at least there are no sky-scratchers.'

I grin. 'You mean skyscrapers.'

'Ah, yes! So sorry,' he says. 'Skyscrapers! *Englisch* is for me difficult. I am learning it only as an adult. As a youth, my second language was *russisch*. There has been little chance to practice either.'

'Your English is very good,' I say. '*Besser als mein deutsch.*'

Our eyes meet. 'Thank you.' He smiles. 'This square is most beautiful at Christmas,' he says. 'The *Weihnachts-markt* is special and here in Erfurt is where it all began - the first Christmas market in Germany. Now they are everywhere.'

'Yes, there's one in Liverpool.'

'Really,' he says. 'So funny to think of such a German thing in England.'

I change the subject. '*Bist du Erfurter?*'

'*Ja*, I am a *Puffbohne*,' he says. 'What means a special

77

type of bean. I know not how to say it in *Englisch*. *Erfurter* are named for this bean, which the population are consuming in the middle ages.'

'I'm a Scouser,' I say. '*Aus* Liverpool. Scouse is a type of stew.'

'Stew?' he asks, creasing his brow.

'*Eintopf*,' I explain.

'Ah, so we are both citizens named for food.'

We eat at a bar-cum-restaurant off the main square. It's rustic with wood panelling and wrought ironwork. We sit opposite each other at a table at a window that looks out on to the street. We're the only diners. A slim, middle-aged waitress with green eyes and a head of orange hair greets us and offers a table. She smiles constantly. '*Was trinken Sie?*' she asks in a high-pitched whine.

Edgar has a beer. I have a mineral water.

We study the menu then I look out on to the street and watch passers-by – a young couple holding hands, an old woman pulling a shopping trolley and a young Muslim woman wearing a hijab and carrying a child. Edgar smiles and makes to say something, but the server returns with our drinks. She takes our food order. We both choose *Rostbrätel*.

'*Mit Pommes oder Bratkartoffeln*?' the waitress asks.

I have the fried potatoes and Edgar has the fries, then, when the waitress has gone, Edgar takes a gulp of beer and places the glass down on the table. He leans

78

forward and smiles at me. 'I am glad we are meeting,' he says. 'You are... *männlich*.'

'Thanks,' I say.

He leans further forward. 'This is important for me.'

'Yes,' I say, nodding. 'I read your profile.'

The waitress returns and Edgar pulls away from me, leaning back into his seat. She lays out the cutlery then leaves us to chat about the weather and football. The local teams, FC Erfurt and archrivals Rot Weiss Jena are in different leagues, but both are struggling.

Our meals arrive and when I take my first mouthful of pork, Edgar asks if it tastes good and I say that it does. He explains that *Rostbrätel* is pork-neck cooked over charcoal and marinated in beer, Thuringian mustard, onions, caraway seeds and pepper. '*Typisch Thüringisch,*' he says. 'Second only to *Bratwurst* I am thinking.'

'It has a lovely sweetness,' I say.

'*Genau*. The duet of onions and beer.'

We eat in silence for a little while then I ask him the question that has been on my mind ever since I arrived in Erfurt. 'Have things changed for the better?'

His face drops. He puts down his cutlery and leans back into his chair. He purses his lips then leans forward, staring at me. 'Often this is the question with you foreigners,' he says. 'It makes me uneasy.'

'Why?' I ask.

'Before the Change things for me were... okay.'

'And you feel uneasy about that?'

Alone with the Germans

'Yes, because *they* want that I should not have been okay,' he says. 'They say that I must be a bad person, but I am not a bad person. I was never a bad person, I loved the DDR, my country, but they are not liking that. Understand?'

I don't understand, not really, but nod anyway. 'What did you do in the DDR?' I ask.

'What did I do?'

'For work,' I say, but he doesn't understand that either. '*Beruflich*?'

'*Ach*! I was twenty-seven when the Change came. I was a policeman.' He watches for something in my face.

'And things are worse now?'

He picks up his knife and fork. 'It is not so easy to explain,' he says. He cuts up his food then, holding his knife and fork as if he might eat me, he stares at me. 'Yes, I think some things are worse, not all things, but altogether, things are worse for me.' He looks down at his plate. He lifts meat to his mouth, which he chews thoroughly.

'But you have freedom, democracy and now your wife is gone you can be your true self.'

He sighs, places his knife and fork back down on the table, but continues to chew. He swallows, takes a mouthful of beer then pats his mouth with his napkin. 'This democracy you mention, this freedom, it brings not all good.' I lean forward a little. 'Outside Erfurt, Weimar, Jena, the big towns where there is *Tourismus*, education

80

and jobs, this land *Thüringen* - Thuringia as you say, *ja*?'

I nod.

'Outside these towns my homeland is dying. Take a train and you see it. Empty houses, empty buildings, empty villages. *Alles leer!* It gives no work for the young and they must leave. Are you not aware of these things?'

'No,' I admit.

'Matthias has no job,' Edgar sighs. 'I worry for him. He spends time with the wrong people. And when you say my 'true self', you mean something of the sexual, but this is not important for me. This is not something I tell people. It is private. Erfurt is not Berlin or Hamburg or Köln. It is a different world. We must be discreet.'

'Would you sooner things had stayed as they were?'

He thinks. '*Ja,*' he says. 'In the old days, I felt safe. We had community. Now everyman is for himself. I think you would find it hard to understand. There were bastards even in the old days. Always complaining, always critical, not for the people and only for themselves, but in those times they were not so many.'

En route to his apartment, we stop at a bakery and Edgar buys cakes. I wait outside. He emerges with a white cardboard box tied up with red ribbon. '*Donauwelle,*' he explains. He leads the way and we don't talk much.

After a few minutes, we arrive at a drab three-storey concrete apartment block. He unlocks the door to the building, invites me in and together we climb the stairs to the first floor. He opens the door to his apartment and we step inside. He instructs me to sit on a bench and remove my shoes then offers me a pair of flip-flops. 'Belonging to Matthias,' he says. They are two or three sizes too big and it's a chore to stop them slipping off my feet.

His apartment is ordinary, old-fashioned. In the living room a *Wandschrank*, a huge cupboard, takes up a whole wall. In amongst the odd ceramic and the many travel books on the shelves there are a series of framed photographs. Most show Edgar, handsome, smiling, a young man in his police uniform. I study them while Edgar gets me a glass of water from the kitchen. He returns and hands me the glass. '*Danke,*' I say. I take a slug. It's cold and tastes of chemicals.

He looks at me, studies my face, smiles. I smile back at him. 'Shall we go to bed?' he says.

Afterwards, we sit in our underwear at the kitchen table. I wear black Calvin Klein briefs and he's in white boxer shorts. We drink filter coffee and eat the *Donauwelle*.

'*Schmeckt gut?*'

'*Ja,*' I say. '*Lecker.*'

Edgar says that he doesn't exactly know why the cake is known as *Donauwelle*, but that the dark and light swirls within the cake look like waves. 'It must be popular with the people along the Donau,' he says, 'that river that you know as the Danube.'

The phone rings. 'I must take this,' he says and as he walks toward the hallway he stops, leans down, looks me in the face then pecks me on the cheek. 'I will be only a moment.' He enters the hallway, closes the door to the kitchen and picks up the receiver.

I eat my cake, slurp my coffee and listen. I hardly catch a word. He replaces the receiver then re-enters the kitchen. He's agitated. 'You must go,' he says.

'Now?'

'*Ja*,' he says. 'Matthias, he comes.'

We return to the bedroom together and pick up our clothes. He dresses quickly then tidies up, readjusts the duvet and checks the floor. He takes an aerosol and sprays fake mountain freshness into the air. Then, when I am dressed, we walk into his hallway together and I sit on the bench, remove the flip-flops and put my shoes on.

'Can we meet again?'

I look up from tying my shoelaces. 'Perhaps.'

'When?'

'I'm not sure, I return to Frankfurt on Tuesday.'

'We have some days then,' he smiles. 'Take my number.' He finds a writing block and a pen then writes his phone number on the top sheet of paper. 'Here,' he says handing it to me. I take it, fold it in half and pocket it without looking at it. Then, when I have pulled my shoes on, I stand up and he hugs me. He kisses me on the neck. '*Danke*,' he says. '*Es war schön*.' He sighs. '*Bis bald.'*

'Bye,' I say and then I walk out of the apartment and down the stairs without looking back.

I am two hundred metres along the street when I notice him walking toward me. He's six or seven centimetres taller than his father. His hair is much shorter than in the photo in Edgar's wallet. Edgar was right about the weight; Matthias is fat, pudgy, round-headed. He wears a black nylon bomber jacket. There's an emblem on the right shoulder, the letters NPD in white within a red circle. The acronym stands for *Nationaldemokratische Partei Deutschlands,* the nationalist party. He catches me staring. He shouts something. A deep, harsh voice. I look away. *'Arschloch,'* he bawls.

I reach the main road. The traffic drowns out his other insults. I walk to the crossing. When the lights change, I walk to the other side. I look back, but he's gone.

As I walk to the hotel, I wonder if the flip-flops will retain my warmth. And if they do, whether Matthias will notice. And if he does, whether he will ask Edgar who had worn them and what Edgar might say.

That evening, I return to the main square. I enter the first restaurant that I find. I take a seat, order a beer then go into my pocket to retrieve the square of paper. He's a neat writer. The numbers are easy to read. I enter them into the address book of my mobile phone.

Beans and Stew

The waiter returns with my beer. '*Etwas zu essen?'*

'*Ja,*' I say and I order beans and stew.

The Last Queen

of Bavaria

'*Jetzt müssen wir gehen,*' Detlev says from the front door. 'Or you will miss your train.'

I look up from the bench where I sit, pulling on my boots. 'Okay, I'm coming,' I say and stand up.

Behind me, Olaf emerges from the kitchen into the hallway smoking a cigarette. '*Ahoi,*' he says and I turn to face him. We smile at each other.

Detlev says something that I don't understand.

'*Na, ja,*' Olaf replies and then, holding the cigarette in his left hand, he offers me his right. I take it and look into his clear, green eyes. His grip is firm. I pull him into me. I peck him on the neck. I breathe in his funk; he smells of garlic and tobacco and sweat, but mostly garlic.

'*Danke,*' I say. '*Es war schön.*'

Detlev watches as Olaf runs his free hand down my back, smoothing down my khaki-coloured, crumpled t-shirt. His hand stops at my coccyx, where he pats me twice. We unhitch then Detlev opens the front door. 'Come on,' he demands.

I follow him outside. The air is cool, turbulent and full of sound. Two woodpigeons, fat and inelegant, coo and flutter in the moving branches above. The wind whimpers and rakes the long grass in the garden. Somewhere, a bee buzzes.

I walk to the Audi then wait as Detlev calls something to Olaf who steps out from behind the front door and takes a long drag on his cigarette. The two Germans exchange a few words. I hear Olaf say, '*Ehemann.*' Detlev pecks him on the lips then walks to the car, opens the door and lowers himself into the driver's seat.

'*Tschüss,*' I say to Olaf.

'*Ciao,*' is his reply.

I climb into the car next to Detlev. He puts the key into the ignition. The dashboard lights up. He looks at me. I hold his stare then wink. He smirks.

'*Warten Sie!*' Olaf suddenly shouts waving his hands at us before he dashes into the house. He emerges seconds later carrying something in a black plastic carrier bag. He approaches my side of the car. Detlev presses a button and the window lowers. '*Ein Geschenk,*' Olaf says. He hands me the bag. I open it. It contains a plastic box, inside it is something wrapped in greaseproof paper. I sniff at it and recognise the pungent, garlicky odour.

'*Kräuterbutter?*' I ask.

Olaf nods. '*Mit Bärlauch.*'

I don't understand.

'Made with bear garlic,' Detlev explains. 'It grows wild along the roads. The taste is garlic, but the flavour is coming from the leaves not the root.'

'*Hausgemacht,*' Olaf says.

'Homemade! *Danke.*'

Olaf bats my thanks away with a wave of his hand. '*Geiler Mann,*' he says. I laugh at the compliment then he pokes his head in through the open window and pecks me on the cheek. '*Wiedersehen,*' he says then withdraws.

The car starts. Detlev presses a button and the window rises. We move away from the house and I wave Olaf goodbye. As we get to the road, I glance in the wing mirror to see him standing, forlorn-looking, watching us disappear. 'Why didn't Olaf come with us?' I ask.

'He has things to do,' Detlev says then checks both ways for traffic. '*Musik?*' he asks. I nod. He presses another button on the dashboard and something electronic and vaguely Gaelic drowns out the sounds of nature.

The road to Suhl is empty. To the east, just above the horizon, the autumn sun makes silhouettes of the pine trees on the ridges of the hills. Above us, on the other side of the road, mist from the summit descends through the tops of the trees. Blue-black crows at the roadside caw and take flight.

Detlev glances at me. 'Do you meet many men online?'

I raise my eyebrows. '*Natürlich,*' I say then reach over and squeeze his knee.

He laughs. '*Schlampe,*' he squeals.

I feign indignation. '*Du Kerl,*' I say. '*Ich bin keine Schlampe... ich bin ein Flittchen!*'

Alone with the Germans

He looks back to the road. '*Ach, die Ironie!*' he laughs. '*Schlampe, Flittchen*, both words for slut,' he says as if I did not know. He turns the music down. 'Erfurt,' he says, after a few seconds, 'is a long way to come for sex. England even further.'

'Perhaps I want more than sex.'

'*Was?*' he demands. 'Love?'

'No, not love.' I smile a half-hearted smile. He nods and does not enquire any further. We sit listening to the dour music for a few minutes until the road starts to descend and the view changes.

'Over there,' Detlev says, indicating a hill with a dip of his head. 'Over there is Bavaria.' I look toward the hill then back at him. His face appears long and thin, his features slight and his scrubbed skin pink and bright, almost luminous. Yet, his lips are pale. I look into his grey-blue eyes and he smiles to reveal uneven, off-white teeth.

'Ah, yes,' I say, 'the border between Thuringia and Bavaria, the fabled *Bratwurst-Weisswurst-Äquator*.'

He laughs and takes a hand from the wheel and briefly squeezes my thigh. 'Why does an Englishman know such very German things?'

'I have an interest in German things.'

'*Wurst* is very German for sure,' he chuckles. 'Which do you prefer *Bratwurst* or *Weisswurst*?'

'*Bratwurst*,' I proclaim.

'And how do you like your *Bratwurst*?'

'Roasted over wood or gas and served with mustard.'

'*Prima, prima!*' he says. 'And I suppose you also know the words of the *Rennsteigleid*.'

'No,' I say. 'Only the melody.' To prove the point, I whistle a few bars of the hymn, a Thuringian anthem. Detlev joins in, but our whistling quickly degenerates into laughter. It takes a minute or so for us to settle down and then Detlev frowns. 'But really,' he says, 'why such interest in Germany?'

I sigh and look through the passenger window at the passing vegetation then stare back at him. 'My father is German.'

'Is he Thuringian?'

'I don't know,' I admit and Detlev turns to me. 'It's possible. I never knew him. My mother refused to talk about him.'

'Nothing at all?'

'They met in Jena,' I say. 'My mother was a British communist. She attended an international conference on something or other. I know that much, but not his name or anything else.'

Detlev draws a deep breath. 'I'm sorry,' he says then looks at the road.

'No need to be.'

We are silent until we reach a village several kilometres further along. We pass through a collection of old buildings – a church, a town hall and some houses with high, red-tiled roofs.

Alone with the Germans

'Hildburghausen,' Detlev announces.

'Is it famous?'

He shakes his head. '*Nein,*' he grunts. 'It is old, hundreds of years for sure, but not so famous.' He begins to say something else, but stops as we approach a sharp bend, which demands his concentration. A few seconds later, after he has negotiated the turn, we are on the road out of the village. He gives me the briefest of glances. 'Hildburghausen is known for just one thing,' he says and looks up at the overhead mirror. 'Therese von Sachsen-Hildburghausen, the last queen of Bavaria was born here.'

'Never heard of her,' I say.

'She is remembered as an exemplary mother and wife. The *Oktoberfest,* the beer festival...' He pauses a moment. '*Ja,* I think the first *Oktoberfest* in München celebrated her marriage to King Ludwig. She was a loyal and moral queen, but Ludwig had many affairs and he was forced to abdicate over his adultery.'

'Interesting,' I say. 'A moral queen.'

'Well,' Detlev smiles, 'all queens have morals of some sort.'

I laugh then moments later, trees line both sides of the road. I look up through the smoked glass sunroof. Something large and predatory, an eagle or a common buzzard perhaps, flies over us. There are no clouds. I turn my eyes to Detlev. 'Did things change much?'

He glances at me. '*Nach der Wende?*'

I nod.

He returns his attention back to the road. 'Yes, of course,' he says. 'Everything changed after eighty-nine. Why do you ask?'

'Just wondered.'

He glances at me again, but avoids my eyes. He draws a deep breath then concentrates on the road. 'I was... It's hard to say in English. *Gefängnis.* Understand?'

'You were in prison!' I turn to face him. The car stops at a crossroads. He glances at me, looks down. I reach over and place my hand on his hand. I squeeze gently.

'It's okay,' he says. 'I can talk about it.'

I withdraw my hand. 'Your crime, was it sexual or something else?'

He gives me a look. 'Political,' he says. 'They cared less what you did with your dick than what you said about Honecker.' He leans forward and looks in both directions. He glances at me, avoids eye contact then drives ahead. 'I was young and I was drunk and I said things. Silly, juvenile things. I was denounced and then questioned, tried and convicted. It was a very efficient process, but at least, they kept me nearby.'

On the other side of the crossroads, he picks up speed. After the forest, there is farmland. Lush, flat and green like England. Large fields with long rows of what might be asparagus.

'It affected us greatly,' Detlev says and looks at me, reading the question in my expression. 'Not Olaf and I,

95

we met later. I mean my family – *Mutti, Vater,* my sister Heike and Georg, my older brother.' He sighs. 'Heike was bright, a science student, she wanted to go to university, but she had a brother who was unpatriotic. These things mattered.' He sighs again, and his eyes stray back to the road. '*Mutti* took it badly. She died aged only fifty-two in this land where women live to eighty or ninety years.'

The road descends and across the valley, the red roofs of Suhl come into view.

'Even to think of it, I used to shake.' He looks in the overhead mirror. 'And then, some years ago, they asked me to talk to the young people. Good kids. Fourteen and fifteen year olds. They had no idea what went on *vor der Wende* as we say.'

'Did it help?'

'Yes,' he says, 'a kind of therapy.'

I nod then lean back into my seat. 'And after prison?'

'Düsseldorf,' he says. 'They threw me away. A new life in the West, but…' He sighs. '*Ich bin Thüringer.* This is my homeland. After eighty-nine, I returned as soon as I could. *Mutti* died within the year.'

We enter the outskirts of Suhl; low-rise, drab buildings either side of the road. After a few streets, we stop at traffic lights. Detlev looks me in the face. He swallows. 'Where they kept me, it is here on the right.' The traffic lights change and about eighty metres further along we approach a side street, he raises a hand from the steering wheel and points. 'There,' he says. 'They kept me there.' I look up toward a huddle of white buildings. In the few seconds it takes to pass, I do not see anything unusual or sinister. No watch towers, no barbed wire fences. The buildings could be offices, apartments, shops and perhaps that is what they have become.

'What happened to the people who did it to you?'

'They are still here,' he says. 'They have moved into other things - security, commerce, non-governmental organisations or even the state government. Nice, steady jobs. I don't see them, but I know that they are here.' Detlev looks at me. 'And they know I am here too.'

We reach the train station. We park up. We get out of the Audi and walk to the platform. It is deserted. The station clock is at 7:49. The train to Erfurt is due at 7:52.

'I am glad that we have met,' Detlev says. 'It was good to practice my English and fuck with you.'

I laugh. *'Ja, ich habe deutsch geübt.'*

'Yes, I think you have used German very well.'

I carry the *Kräuterbutter* and we walk to the ticket machine. Detlev helps me, expertly working the touch-screen. A ticket costs twelve Euros and fifty cents. I feed in a blue twenty Euro note. The machine accepts it then the internal printer whirrs into action and coins clank. I stoop down to collect my change and the ticket from the drawer. I step away from the machine, look at the ticket and pocket the coins. *'Danke,'* I say.

'You would get the ticket without my help.'

Alone with the Germans

'I mean *danke* for last night, this morning and what you told me on the journey.' He smiles. I open my arms. He closes his eyes. His body, warm and hard, yet pneumatic, envelops me. '*Danke*,' I whisper. I let go and he steps back. 'We should keep in touch,' I say.

He nods. 'Yes, we can chat online and perhaps meet again.'

'Perhaps,' I say as the train enters the station.

'And perhaps without Olaf,' he says. His eyes scan my face for a reaction.

'*Auf Wiedersehen*,' I say.

'*Auf Wiedersehen*,' he replies and turns to leave.

'Oh, Detlev,' I call when the train has stopped. 'What was her name?'

He looks back along the platform toward me. His eyes narrow. 'Who do you mean?'

'That moral queen,' I say. 'The last queen of Bavaria.'

Canaletto

Vernon's father never considered himself a teutophobe. Of course, he would never have used that word - he would have simply said German-hater. He maintained that he did not hate all Germans; he hated only one German. Yet, whilst watching tennis on TV he would always support the player opposing Steffi Graf or Boris Becker or, years later, Roger Federer - even though Federer was Swiss and not German. The only German that Vernon's father claimed to hate was a woman. Her name was Elke. Elke was the first wife of Gerald, Vernon's paternal grandfather.

Elke and Gerald met during the War in Hameln, *die Rattenfängerstadt* – the town in the fairytale about the Pied Piper. Terrified and conflicted, the seventeen-year-old Elke had jumped into the River Weser convinced that the invading Allied troops would shoot the men then rape and murder the women. Gerald was a British soldier. He saw Elke jump. He unloaded his kit and went in to the river after her. She wanted to drown, but the river was shallow and he was strong. Gerald dragged her to safety and later, he persuaded her that everything would be fine, that he would protect her and that life, no matter

101

what road it took, was worth living. Elke was beautiful. Gerald was handsome. They fell in love. It was inevitable. They married in England a year after the War.

Things did not end well. Gerald's family, friends and neighbours were hostile toward Elke - 'That Hun girl.' Elke grew homesick too. For a while, they could not find work. Money was tight. There were constant rows. Then, quite suddenly, Elke met another man. Elke and Gerald divorced, but Gerald never got over her. A few years later, Gerald married Winnie, Vernon's grandmother, and when Vernon's father was five years old, Elke died. She drowned in the Thames estuary in what *The Evening Standard* described as 'an unfortunate circumstance'.

'After that funeral,' Vernon's father once explained to his teenage son, 'Dad was never the same. He'd loved your gran and me, but he stopped loving us when that woman was put into the ground.'

Following Elke's death, Gerald drank heavily and cried a lot and that pretty much described the rest of his life, which ended when he was just forty-seven.

Despite his father's teutophobia, Vernon grew up to be the complete opposite. His father blamed his mother for what he called Vernon's 'German thing.' He maintained that she had told the six-year-old Vernon about the 'fairytale love affair in the fairytale town.' Yet, Vernon had no recollection of his mother having ever mentioned Elke. No, Vernon's 'German thing' started with a pubescent introduction to Kraftwerk and German electronic music. In adolescence, he developed an interest in history that led him to the discovery of the Weimar Republic. At school, when he was thirteen years of age, he dropped French and took up German. Then the sixteen-year-old Vernon found the novels and biographies of Christopher Isherwood. In his final years of school, he excelled at both history and German. He went on to take a degree in German at university then at twenty-two, he moved to Germany to take up a job in Berlin.

Eventually, his father's view of Germans, including Elke, mellowed. His views on most things mellowed. This also included his view on his son's sexuality, something that he accepted, but found difficult to discuss.

Vernon's father's change in outlook had a lot to do with what he claimed was an end to running his life on his own self-will. Occasionally, he indicated to Vernon that he thought that all things happened for a reason and that reason was God's Will. Everyone (Vernon, his sister – Jacqueline, and various aunts, uncles and cousins) considered this religiosity to be a reaction to the death of Vernon's mother. It was also about growing old and coming to terms with death.

A by-product of his father's faith was an interest in church architecture. In his final years, he would often visit local churches, and in the summer when the weather was good and his health allowed, he would visit cathedrals and churches further afield. He especially liked the grandeur of St Paul's, but also the massive arches and stained glass windows of the Cathedral Church of the Risen Christ otherwise known as the Liverpool Anglican Cathedral. The family home became full of pictures and paintings of churches, those that he had visited and others. Among them was one by the artist Canaletto. Both Vernon and his father greatly admired it. It was different to the other pictures in that it was not a view of a single building, but a cityscape depicting a river and a bridge and many church spires. It hung in the dining room. Sometimes, when Vernon was back home from Germany visiting his father, he would find himself in the dining room searching for something or other and he would stand and look at the Canaletto, taking in the spires and the clouds and the sky as if he was there, wherever there might be. The print bore the name Canaletto, but no other information. Vernon and his father presumed that it was a scene from renaissance Italy, Florence or Ravenna perhaps.

Vernon's father died on a Wednesday. Earlier that day, Vernon received a call on his mobile phone as his train pulled into Dresden *Hauptbahnhof*. A well-spoken female office junior informed him that the meeting, which he had travelled from Berlin to attend, would not be possible. Herr Crott, the contact he was due to meet, had been taken ill and, because the company was small and taking part in a major trade fair, there was no one else to take his place. Vernon said that he would contact Herr Crott to reschedule then thanked the young woman and hung up. The train journey had taken three hours. A waste of time to go straight back to Berlin, especially as it was his first visit to Dresden. It was not sightseeing weather though - fine rain and a driving wind. Sitting at a table in a coffee shop in the station, he googled something on his mobile phone then, after checking several websites, he went outside and climbed into a taxi. 'Friedensstraße *bitte,'* he said to the driver.

A few minutes later, the taxi pulled up outside Man's Paradise. Vernon paid the driver and entered the premises. A cute, smiling twenty-something welcomed him, took the entrance fee then issued him with a towel, locker key and flip-flops. In the changing room, Vernon stripped, put his clothes in a locker and showered before wrapping himself in the towel. He strolled into the lounge, where the same assistant stood behind a counter singing along to a Helene Fischer video. There were only two other men in the place. Both were German and like Vernon, in their thirties. Johann was slim and tall with green eyes, fair hair and a goatee beard. However, Vernon found the other man to be both more attractive than Johann and similar to himself; tall, broad-shouldered, dark-haired and brown-eyed.

Still, Johann was more than happy to chat. The other man grunted something in a thick Saxon accent - he did not intend to reveal any personal details about himself. Vernon and Johann exchanged puzzled looks. The man's reluctance to give his name, however, was not a deal-breaker when it came to sex, which Vernon saw as the reflection of some sort of *Zusammengehörigskeitgefühl*; a sense or feeling of a common bond that existed between them.

Afterwards, the man with no name said `*Ciao*,' but not `*Danke*' and left. Johann and Vernon sat in the lounge, ordered coffee and chatted. Johann, a music teacher, lived in Leipzig with his mother. He wanted to move to Berlin, but lamented that there were no jobs. Well, there were jobs, just none that paid well enough to warrant the move. Vernon lived in Berlin and worked as a contract manager for an events management company.

They were both single.

They were both lonely.

They were both open to possibilities.

Unfortunately, Vernon had to return to Berlin.

In the changing room, they dressed then hugged. They swapped mobile phone numbers. They returned their towels and flip-flops then paid for their coffee. Outside, the weather had improved and rather than catch a taxi, Vernon decided to head to the local train station to catch the connecting train to the *Hauptbahnhof*. Johann walked to a friend's apartment nearby. Moments after they parted on Friedensstraße, Vernon turned to see Johann standing and watching him. He smiled and waved. '*Ruf mich an*,' he hollered to the German gesturing with his thumb and pinkie.

Leipzig. *Heldenstadt;* the city of heroes. Johann's mother lived her entire life there. Like her son, she was a teacher, but taught German as opposed to music. Johann's father was a manager at a large bakery. He drank a lot and left Johann's mother when she told him that she was pregnant. She never ever saw him again. She did not agree with abortion and prepared to raise the child herself. Her parents, as ever, were critical. They offered little help and then, when Johann was a toddler, they died in a car crash shortly after taking possession of the 'Trabi' that they had waited a decade to own. Fortunately, her friends were there for her and despite the many faults of the German Democratic Republic, childcare provision was not one of them. She worked and looked after herself and her son.

In the late eighties, after Johann celebrated his *Jugendweihe,* his mother became heavily involved in the church. It had something to do with the *Jugendweihe* itself; a coming of age celebration that lacked any religious element. She would have preferred Johann to have followed a more religious route, but he was resistant to the idea of Confirmation and she was not the kind of Christian to force her views on others especially her intelligent, precocious son. It also had to do with a new vitality within her church, the *Nikolaikirche*. In addition to observing Sundays and festivals, she began attending the regular Monday evening Peace Prayers. She encouraged Johann to attend too, but he would have none of it. She was not an overtly political woman, but her involvement in the Monday Peace Prayers led her to take part in the demonstrations. She always focused on peace and carried a banner bearing the phrase '*Kein Gewalt'* - which the crowd would shout when there was any confrontation with the authorities.

Johann's mother never thought of herself as a heroine even though she had attended the Monday Peace Prayers from the very beginning. Her part in the *Leipziger Herbst*, the autumn that changed everything, was small. She was one of the seven thousand crammed into the *Nikolaikirche* when several hundred Stasi officers came to break-up the meeting. The pastor asked the officers to join the congregation, to listen and miracle! They did.

Later that night, like tens of thousands of others on the streets, she defied the order not to march. The State expected violence, but the People offered only candles and prayers. The State with its riot gear, helmets, guns and tanks could not fight that. It failed to stop the marchers and that night the fate of the regime was sealed. The Revolution would be peaceful – *das Friedliche Revolution*. It would succeed. It was inevitable.

If the results of the Revolution were disappointing, Johann's mother never let it show. She got on with her life. She worked hard, looked after Johann and prayed.

Canaletto

After 1989, amongst the objects that adorned their apartment were photographs from the Revolution and the *Kein Gewalt* banner, framed and hung in the living room. There were many religious paintings and views of churches too. Among them was one by Canaletto. It hung in the hall opposite the coat rack and above the bench where Johann, his mother and visitors sat to change their shoes whenever entering or leaving the apartment.

Twenty minutes after leaving Johann, Vernon received a call on his mobile phone. He was at Neustadt station waiting for the connecting train to the *Hauptbahnhof*. It began to rain. He hoped that the caller would be Johann, but it was not him.

'Hi, Vern,' Jacqueline said. 'There's no other way to do this, I just have to say it.'

'Say what?' he asked

'Dad,' she said, her voice cracking. 'He's dead.'

Their father had died an hour before she phoned. He had the flu. He was admitted into hospital the previous evening. 'Just as a precaution,' the doctor had said and because of that, Jacqueline had not wanted to worry Vernon. At ten that morning, however, she received the phone call; their father's condition had deteriorated. He was unconscious, barely breathing. She arrived at the hospital just before eleven. He died a little after twelve while she held his hand. He did not regain consciousness.

Alone with the Germans

Shocked and disorientated, she was unable to call Vernon until that moment.

'Are you alright?' Jacqueline said. 'Say something!'

Yet, Vernon could not say anything. He looked up and out of the station. In the distance, high and black and sharp, he saw a church spire. 'I'm okay, I'll call you back,' he said.

Vernon exited the station. He headed toward the spire. The rain stopped as he made his way up the incline and he began to see the full-scale of the church, the *Dreikönigskirche*, the Church of the Three Magi. It was a large, formidable, solid building. The kind of church that Vernon knew his father would have admired. As he neared it, he heard organ music. He entered the building and walked to the nave. He took a seat in the white space and stared up at a golden angel. In the gallery above, an organist played Bach and the still-beautiful remnant of Benjamin Thomae's magnificent marble Baroque altar (that had been severely damaged in the Allied bombings of 1945) was before him. Vernon sucked at his bottom lip for a long while then he sighed and quietly began to sob. An elderly woman next to him patted him on the shoulder. '*Gott ist gut*,' she whispered. '*Gott ist barmherzig*.' Yet, God was not, as far Vernon was concerned, good or merciful.

Eventually, the organist stopped playing and the congregation left. Vernon was alone. His mobile phone rang. He thought that it would be Jacqueline, but it was not Jacqueline. It was Johann. Vernon told him what had happened. Johann said that he would be with him presently. 'You don't have to come,' Vernon said.

'Yes, I do,' Johann replied and when he arrived a few minutes later, Vernon was standing at the church entrance. They hugged and stood holding each other. 'Do you want to go somewhere?' Johann asked after a little while.

'No,' Vernon said. Yet, without speaking, they climbed the stairs of the church tower. Johann paid the few Euros to go to the top. At the viewing platform, they stepped out and looked out over Dresden and... gift! Vernon recognised the shapes of some of the buildings – the dome of the *Frauenkirche*, certainly, and the spikes of the *Schlossturm* and the cathedral. Other spires were missing and there were newer ones - the *Kreuzkirche* and the *Rathaus.* He knew what he was looking at though. 'Oh, God,' he said. 'Canaletto!'

Johann turned to him. 'You know this view too?'

'The question that we ask is this,' Vernon said. 'During their life did he or she do the best that they could?'

Up until that point, Vernon had been in control, but then there was something, he was not sure what it was exactly - something to do with the faces staring back at him perhaps or just a sudden spike of grief, which caused him to falter. He recomposed himself though. He swallowed, drew breath then continued. 'With respect to

Dad,' he said. 'I can state categorically, that the answer is yes.'

Back at the house, after the internment of his father's body in the graveyard, Vernon sat in the dining room with Jacqueline and various other relatives and family friends. Jacqueline had cleared the room of clutter the previous evening to make space for the buffet. Vernon looked at the Canaletto, which still hung on the wall and he told Jacqueline that he did not care much about how things were shared out between them, but that he was taking the Canaletto print with him when he returned to Germany. She offered no objection; she had never really liked it and it held little (if any) monetary or emotional worth to her whatsoever.

The rescheduled meeting with Herr Crott did not go well. In hindsight, Vernon realised that he lacked energy and his presentation had been lacklustre. Jacqueline had probably been right, Vernon should have allowed himself more time before returning to work. Even so, the reason that Vernon's company did not get 'the gig' (as Vernon called the events that he managed) was down to budget; a local firm entered a cheaper bid.

Still, after the meeting, he met with Johann for lunch at a Russian cafe near to the *Zwinger Palast*. 'How are you?' Johann asked.

'Not great,' Vernon admitted and they sat and ate their soup and talked not just about Vernon's father, but also work and Johann's ambitions to move to Berlin.

'I'm glad we met,' Johann said.

'Me too,' Vernon agreed.

They both wondered what had happened to the other guy in Man's Paradise. 'He was strange,' Johann said.

'But good-looking,' Vernon added.

'*Ja, sehr geil.*'

Eventually, Vernon had to go. Johann accompanied him to the *Hauptbahnhof*. 'You must visit me,' Vernon said.

'I will,' Johann promised. They hugged then Vernon took his seat on the train. As it pulled away, Johann gestured and mouthed something; '*Ruf mich an.*'

Johann's mother was not looking forward to meeting her son's lover. He was, after all, responsible for taking Johann away from her. Johann had been in Berlin for just three months, but she had lost him long before that. She viewed Vernon as an interloper. She also considered the English similar to the Americans - not as loud, but just as arrogant. Yet, when she met him, she found that her son's lover was a quiet, humble man. She had envisioned him as being slight, fey, effeminate even. Yet, he was tall and solid with wide shoulders and a deep voice. He also possessed an openness that was hard not to like. She could see why Johann loved Vernon, an insight that shocked her, because she realised love is love and that as Johann said, she just had to get over 'the gay thing'.

Alone with the Germans

Vernon was also genuinely interested in her faith and the *Nikolaikirche* in a way that Johann had never been. He was a little nervous too and there was a moment when he referred to the Revolution as *niedlich* instead of *friedlich*, which caused all of them to laugh. 'A cute revolution,' Johann said. 'So much better than a peaceful one.'

There was one thing that might have caused concern, the pause that accompanied the look between the two men when Johann's mother asked Vernon how they had met. Yet, if she noticed, she never let it show, and his answer (that they had met at a cafe near to the *Frauenkirche* when he was on a business trip) chimed with what Johann had previously told her.

'Take care of him,' she said when Johann was in the kitchen making coffee.

'I will,' Vernon said and she did not doubt him.

The anniversary of Vernon's father's death fell in the same week as Johann's mother's birthday. And some years, Vernon and Johann visit Leipzig. They kennel Mops, their dog - a pug that Vernon wanted to call Pug, but which Johann persuaded him to call Mops (German for pug). And they drive from Berlin, where they live in an apartment off the Schönhauser Allee.

In Leipzig, they stay with Johann's mother in Johann's old room. On the day of her birthday, they take her for lunch at *Auerbach's Keller* and in the evening, they may take in a concert at the *Gewandhaus* or the *Thomaskirche*.

On the morning of the anniversary of his father's death (which is also the anniversary of the couple's first meeting), Vernon visits a church or other historic building with Johann before they have lunch. After lunch, they go to the *Dreikönigskirche,* where (if there is one) they may take in an organ recital.

Later, they always climb the stairs of the church tower. On the viewing platform, they look out over Dresden and see something of what Canaletto saw. And there, looking at the spires and the clouds and the sky, Vernon remembers his parents, while Johann thinks of his mother. They think of each other too. Sometimes Vernon thinks how Gerald could not live whilst knowing that Elke was no longer in the world and he wonders how he would fare without Johann. Sometimes Johann thinks about his life in Berlin; how it would have never been possible without the Revolution. Sometimes one or both of them think about Man's Paradise and the man with no name. Yet, no matter whatever else they think about, they are always mindful of their parents' view; that things happen for a reason and that reason is God's Will.

Acknowledgements and Thanks

I wish to acknowledge the *Polari Literary Journal*, (Melbourne, Australia) for publishing an earlier version of 'shaun-how-sir-alley'.

Thanks to the staff and students on the Distance Learning MA in Creative Writing at Lancaster University (2012/14) for their encouragement and feedback.

Similarly, thanks go to Steve Benson and the regulars at the Merseyside LGBT Creative Writing Group.

I also extend my heartfelt appreciation to Philip Heaton, a very patient fellow.

I am fortunate to have met and got to know many inspiring German men and women: Michael M., Ulli, Stephan, Olaf, Frau Doktor, Axl, Niels, Christina, Connie, Jürgen, Eddi, André, Helmut, Steffen, Chris and Michael. *Ich weiss gar nicht, wie ich Ihnen für Ihre Hilfe und Freundshaft danken soll. Sie sind super!*

CPSIA information can be obtained at www.ICGtesting.com
Printed in the USA
LVOW10s1611050516

486862LV00039B/483/P